"You're Planning To Kiss Me Again. And I'm Afraid I Might Kiss You Back."

If that happened, and things got out of hand then turned irretrievably sour, Shelby would have no one to blame but herself.

That night when their lips had brushed, time had wound down, hormones had sat up and, for that moment, the urge to surrender it all had been hypnotic. They'd barely kissed and yet never in her life had she felt that level of raw sexual need. She'd been gripped so soon, so tight, her reaction afterward had been just as fierce.

Reaching forward, she swept the bag off the floor. "I don't want to complicate things."

As Dex came to stand before her, those wonderful, frightening feelings sparked again. When his fresh male scent slipped into her lungs, she held her breath and skirted around him.

Leaning back against the lounge, he crossed his arms and ankles. Relaxed. In control. Insufferable…and irresistible.

Dear Reader,

Welcome to the second installment of The Hunter Pact series where you'll meet—and fall in love with—the brother with a laid-back, playboy bent…Dex Hunter.

Back in Sydney, Australia, the life of Dex's father—legendary media mogul Guthrie Hunter—is still in danger. While leads relating to those assassination attempts are being followed, for safety's sake, the youngest of the clan has been ferried far away. Moviemaking boss Dex is excited to have his little brother come stay in Hollywood.

One problem. He needs a babysitter—pronto. Someone reliable, who adores energetic five-year-old boys. Straight-shooter Shelby Scott seems the perfect choice…and for more than one reason. Dex believes Shelby might be the hottest woman he has ever met. However, he is determined not to get romantically involved with his nanny, no matter how tempting.

After an embarrassing incident she can never live down, Shelby left her small hometown of Mountain Ridge, Oklahoma, to find a brand-new life in L.A. Making do in a waitressing position until something better comes along, Shelby can't believe her luck when one of the regulars needs a live-in to mind his little brother for a spell. It isn't long before Shelby doubts her decision. Sexy Dex Hunter is a lady magnet. Worse, he's proving irresistible to currently down-on-men Shelby, as well. When Shelby plans to duck back to Mountain Ridge to check on her ailing father, she envisages her visit as an ultra-private affair. However, when Dex accompanies her, their steamy secret love affair breaks out into the open. All kinds of ghosts and regrets from both sides of their pasts start to boil and bubble up, too.

I hope you enjoy Dex and Shelby's journey toward their happily-ever-after! Stay tuned for the third brother Wynn Hunter's story coming soon.

Best wishes,

Robyn

Robyn loves to hear from her readers at www.robyngrady.com and on Twitter @robyngrady.

ROBYN GRADY

TEMPTATION ON HIS TERMS

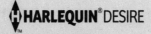

Recycling programs
for this product may
not exist in your area.

ISBN-13: 978-0-373-73256-2

TEMPTATION ON HIS TERMS

Copyright © 2013 by Robyn Grady

This is a work of fiction. Names, characters, places and incidents are
either the product of the author's imagination or are used fictitiously, and
any resemblance to actual persons, living or dead, business establishments,
events or locales is entirely coincidental.

This edition published by arrangement with Harlequin Books S.A.

For questions and comments about the quality of this book, please contact us
at CustomerService@Harlequin.com.

® and TM are trademarks of Harlequin Enterprises Limited or its corporate
affiliates. Trademarks indicated with ® are registered in the United States Patent
and Trademark Office, the Canadian Trade Marks Office and in other countries.

Printed in U.S.A.

ROBYN GRADY

was first published with Harlequin in 2007. Her books have since featured regularly on bestseller lists and at award ceremonies, including a National Readers' Choice Award, a Booksellers' Best Award, CataRomance Reviewers' Choice Award and Australia's prestigious Romantic Book of the Year Award.

Robyn lives on Queensland's beautiful Sunshine Coast with her real-life hero husband and three daughters. When she can be dragged away from tapping out her next story, Robyn visits the theater, the beach and the mall (a lot!). To keep fit, she jogs (and shops) and dances with her youngest to Hannah Montana.

Robyn believes writing romance is the best job on the planet and she loves to hear from her readers. So drop by www.robyngrady.com and pass on your thoughts!

This book is dedicated to my wonderful father,
who was always a hero in my life, as well as in the lives
of so many others. Love you, Jack.

One

Shelby Scott glared at the spectacle unfolding in front of the world-famous hotel and pursed her lips. With amused people skirting by, Dex Hunter was going all-out, kissing—or was that mauling?—one extremely enthusiastic lady. The blaze from her diamanté dress could help bring home a ship in a gale. A starlet wannabe, Shelby surmised, given that Mr. Hunter owned his very own movie studio.

When they'd met earlier that day—after she'd splashed hot coffee all over his shirt cuff—Shelby had promised herself that waitressing was only a stopgap. New to California, she had her heart set on finding a good nanny position. She had experience and everyone back home knew she loved kids. As luck would have it, Mr. Hunter was in the market.

A busy bachelor and head of Hunter Productions, Dex needed a suitable someone to help care for his little brother who was due to pay a solo visit. When Dex learned that child care was her vocation of choice, he'd seemed interested. Then he'd discovered that she'd read every book in the boy's best-loved children's series and even knew the difference between a stegosaurus and a *T. rex*. Apparently his brother *loved* dinosaurs.

Dex said he felt as if he'd struck gold. She'd felt the same way. Because he'd been short on time, they'd agreed to meet tonight to talk more and hopefully finalize the deal.

But the cheap display she was witnessing now quashed any chance of them working together. When his five-year-old brother arrived from Australia, Dex Hunter could make other arrangements. She'd had enough of dealing with Casanova types. In Hollywood or Mountain Ridge, Oklahoma, in blue jeans or tailored trousers...

Hell, they were all the same.

The snap-lock kiss finally broke apart. Dex Hunter's focus shifted and, as if guided by radar, landed smack-dab on Shelby. While she watched, he set the clearly giddy woman aside then strode past two awnings and straight up to Shelby. Over the scent of coming rain, his fresh musky scent filled her lungs at the same time his masculine presence enveloped her. Broad through the shoulders and tall—even compared to her five-foot-ten-inch frame—tonight he exuded a born-to-bed confidence.

But his lidded, tawny-colored gaze was the kicker. Beneath the streetlights, those eyes might be mistaken for a lion's...an intelligent, potentially dangerous beast's.

"You're early," he said, straightening his collar.

"I'm sure I'm right on time." Shelby couldn't help herself. "Are you in the habit, Mr. Hunter, of making a downright show of yourself in public?"

His eyebrows knitted together before he caught on and threw a glance over a jacketed shoulder. One corner of his mouth curved with a grin.

"She did kind of pounce, didn't she?"

"Oh, and he palms off responsibility, too."

His gaze sharpened, then he dragged a finger and thumb down each side of his mouth. When his hand lowered, his jaw was tight and his grin was rubbed clean away. "We've gotten off on the wrong foot."

"We're not *getting off* at all."

Finished and done, she headed for the nearest bus stop.

She'd been in Los Angeles two weeks. Other than a few days in Oklahoma City years ago, she hadn't set foot outside of her hometown before. She'd only settled on California because of a much-loved old movie where the heroine, who had needed a new start, had lucked out when she'd ended up here. Now, feeling alone—and naive—the idea of buckling and going back to "familiar" surged up to grip her like a vise. She had a lifetime of memories in Mountain Ridge—mostly good.

Some seriously bad.

Which was why she'd made that promise to stay away and stay strong. She refused to endure pitying or even disapproving looks from folk she'd known all her life. And if some said that was running away, if there were people who dared imply that was yellow...well, who gave a fat fairy's—

She heard the slap of footfalls on the pavement behind her. Next minute, Dex Hunter reappeared, his dynamo frame physically blocking her this time.

"You said you'd have dinner with me," he said, "to discuss my proposition."

"If that's how you conduct yourself in public while expecting company, I don't care to know what you'd get up to in the privacy of your own home, whether an innocent little boy was staying or not." She tipped forward, spoke clearly. "I won't be a part of it."

"That woman's a friend."

"That would be a friend with benefits?"

"We were saying goodbye."

"I might be a country girl," Shelby drawled, "but I didn't fall off the back of a hay cart yesterday. That embrace was not a friendly farewell."

It was a prelude to something much deeper. Burning, desperate. She'd come across that kind of kiss before.

"Bernice had too much to drink," he told her, catching up as she set off again, a single stride of his equaling two purposeful steps from her. "She's meeting some buddies and wanted me to tag along. When I said I had plans…" He scratched his ear. "Well, she tried to convince me."

"And you put up such a fight," Shelby said prettily.

"For all you know, she might've been my girlfriend. A fiancée even."

At the mention of the *F*-word, Shelby's stomach swooped and she stopped. Dex Hunter couldn't take a hint, even when it slapped him upside the head.

"I didn't like what I saw." Didn't like the way it made her feel. Uncomfortable. Vulnerable. "Call a nanny agency. And, for heaven's sake, wipe that lipstick off your cheek."

"I checked out your references this afternoon," he said. "Got some people on the phone."

Shelby felt her gaze widen, her throat constrict.

"At the café," he said, using a handkerchief to scrub that smear from his jaw, "you mentioned a couple places you worked for back home. People spoke highly of you and your capabilities, by the way. Mrs. Fallon from Hatchlings Kindergarten was especially impressed. She said you connect particularly well with boys."

"I liked roping more than tea parties growing up," she admitted as her thoughts raced on. She didn't mind that he'd followed up on those names she'd supplied, but now she couldn't help but wonder. Who else had Dex Hunter spoken to? What else did he know? Not that he would give a hoot about that ugly incident last month. The episode Mountain Ridge would whisper about and lament for years to come.

"I haven't seen my youngest brother in six months," he was saying, "but I'm sure he's the same kid. Full of mischief and ideas and buckets of energy. You'd like him." A fond smile reflected in those tawny-colored eyes. "Everyone does."

Shelby released a breath.

Okay. She was curious. Had his brother sat in a saddle yet?

Did he like checkers or baseball? Maybe he was more into building blocks, constructing little towns and surrounding them with farms, barns, horses, cows…

Shelby straightened.

None of that erased this man's lame excuse for the nearly R-rated scene she'd just witnessed. Friend indeed.

She crossed her arms. "You'll find someone else."

"I want you."

"Please, just go and join your—"

Midsentence, she'd glanced back. And froze.

The woman—Bernice—had flung her arms around yet *another* man. As her new victim gently pried her away, Bernice tottered then—*oh, dear Lord*—crumpled and began to cry. While Shelby's heart sank, two women rushed up. With arms linked around Bernice's waist, the friends Dex Hunter had mentioned carefully led her away.

"Bernice's fiancé broke off their engagement the other week," he said. "I've known the guy for years. Not the marrying kind. Guess tonight, before she went home for good, Bernice wanted to prove something to the world. To herself. Not that she needs to. She was always too good for Mac."

Knots filled Shelby's stomach. How very much she felt for that woman. Hurt and despair could lead a person to do some seriously dumb things. Things you could barely make sense of later on and never take back.

Dex's voice broke into her thoughts. "This town's too tough for someone like her. Too tough for a lot of people."

Shelby felt his evaluating gaze on her again, before he straightened both shoulders and got back on track.

"Whatever you decide about the job," he said, "I still want to take you to dinner. You've been working, serving people all day. Bet you're as hungry as I am, and I could eat a horse."

She gave a grudging grin. "Sounds as if Mrs. Fallon at the kindergarten mentioned my appetite."

He chuckled, a smooth rich sound that left her feeling as if she were swirling in a pool of deep warm water. Or was that quicksand?

"Tate has an appetite, too," he said. "Last time we caught up, cheeseburgers were his favorite fillers. Although I might have had something to do with that."

Her smile, and opinion of Mr. Hunter, loosened up more. He really was charming. And persuasive. A tricky combination, as past experience had taught her. Still…

"Guess there's no harm in sharing a meal," she said. "But we're going Dutch."

"No need—"

"I insist."

Dex didn't mistake Shelby Scott's tone. The clear-cut message in her words or in her eyes. She would have dinner with him. Might even answer more questions about her nanny experience in Mountain Ridge. Given that their misunderstanding regarding Bernice had been sorted, no reason he and Shelby shouldn't get back to negotiations. Although he wasn't convinced that she saw it that way.

She had a point. Most people would simply call the best nanny agency in town, let them do the screening and save themselves the trouble. But his gut said Shelby Scott was the right person to help care for the little guy, who not only meant more to Dex than anyone in the world but also needed his protection.

Someone wanted to harm their media mogul father. Until that man was brought to justice, Tate needed a safe place to stay. No member of the Hunter clan would take a chance on the five-year-old being caught up in another incident like the one Sydney authorities were investigating now. After being run off the road then, later, shot at, his father had been assaulted and almost abducted. Tate had been with his dad and had been a whisker away from being kidnapped, too.

As Dex swept his gaze up and down the boulevard, deciding on the ideal place to dine—cozy and quiet without being too intimate—his cell phone buzzed. When he ignored it, Shelby seemed confused.

"That could be important," she said.

"We're on our way to dinner."

"Where I come from, it's rude to ignore a ringing phone or a knock at the door."

He considered her big frank green eyes. This wasn't the time to tell her that, in L.A. at least, people ignored phones all the time.

Dex answered the call.

On the other end of the line, his scriptwriter Rance Loggins blurted out, "It's not working. You want Jada to confront Pete at the wedding, but I don't think she should. It's too predictable."

"You'll work something out. Sleep on it."

"I thought you wanted this script finished."

Dex flicked a glance Shelby's way. She stood patiently, looking like a blend of angel and seductress in a pretty pink dress, glossy hair bouncing under its own weight and a warm breeze.

"Dex?" Rance interrupted his thoughts. "You there?"

"Swing by the office—"

"I'm out of town for a week starting tomorrow. It's a pivotal scene." Rance must have heard him push out a breath. "I'm only repeating what you told me. You want it right and you want it quick. This is all that's holding us up."

Hunter Productions had enjoyed a record opening weekend with their most recent release, *Easy Prey,* an action flick featuring one of the day's biggest box office stars. Dex had other movies coming out but he had a good feeling about this one. The characterization was genius. He smelled smash hit. Awards.

Dex eyed Shelby again, caught the time on his watch. Right at seven. Two steaks, desserts, a bottle of wine, cat in the bag…

"I'll be over after ten," he told Rance.

Silence echoed in his ear.

"You're fobbing this off because of a woman," Rance said.

"No, I'm not." *Not in the usual sense.*

"I thought you were committing yourself to building Hunter Productions back up. Making it strong again."

Dex had known Rance a long time. He counted this man as a friend. Now Dex's jaw clenched and voice lowered. He was laid-back, certainly. That didn't translate into pushover.

"You're forgetting who pays the bills," he let his friend know.

"You need to make the cash to pass it on."

Dex ended the call. With her own phone, Shelby was taking shots of the famous fashion shops on Rodeo Drive across the way.

"You need to cancel, don't you?" she said, phone near her face as she clicked. "That's fine. In fact, it's best."

Flicking back his jacket hem, Dex set his hands low on his belt. Damned if he'd let her get away that easily. If for some reason she gave notice at the café, he might never find her again. But Rance had a point.

While he'd refused to spend his life hunched over a desk at the office, until this latest hit, Hunter Productions' books had favored the lean side. When he'd first come out here from Australia, a kid of twenty-five, a friend at the time had helped him with manipulating budgets. He'd learned a lot from Joel Chase, and had put in the kind of crazy hours his family might have trouble believing of him. Even so, if he had to tend to business tonight, he wouldn't let this other important matter slide.

"Come along," he suggested. "We'll grab a bite afterward."

"I'm not comfortable with that."

"Why not?"

"I don't know you well enough."

"I don't own a wooden club, Shelby. I won't knock you out and drag you away to my secret lair."

Her gaze held his with a narrowed pondering look that said she wasn't so sure. She was wary and, living in a place like L.A., wary was good. If she was cautious about going to some unknown address, it only showed common sense. Another plus.

He'd lay the rest on the table.

"My writer's hit a snag with a script," he explained. "The story's a romantic comedy with an edge. We're working on a pivotal scene where everything falls apart. The man who the female lead once loved—a man who cheated on her—is getting married to her friend and she's invited to the wedding. Her date for the evening had to bow out so she's gone on her own."

The single line forming between Shelby's brows suggested that she was intrigued so he went on.

"She's sitting with a group of the bride's relatives, who go on about how beautiful the bride looks in her gown. Then a clumsy waiter spills cucumber soup on the female lead's dress." When Shelby blinked, maybe remembering the splashed coffee incident earlier that day, he continued. "In her stained gown, she's on her way to the restroom, asking herself why she's putting herself through all this, when she runs into the groom."

Shelby waited. "Then what?"

"We're not sure."

Exhaling, she glanced around at the same time she absently dropped her cell in her tote. A Santa Ana wind chose that moment to whirl around their feet, up their legs and into her bag. The gust picked up a loose paper—a card of some sort. Twirling out from the tote, it circled midair then swept toward the road.

Shelby snatched at it. Missed. Without thinking, she stepped off the curb at the precise moment a gleaming new V-8 sedan whooshed past.

Two

Dex leaped forward. At the same instant, the gust from the vehicle—or, perhaps, her own fear—propelled Shelby back onto the curb. Off balance, she smacked into him, then toppled sideways toward the pavement. Before she hit concrete, he caught her in a dramatic low-slanted pose.

While she lay stiff at a thirty-degree angle, his arms suspending her weight, Dex found himself studying her face. Her eyes, fixed and round with fright, were actually the most unusual mint-green mixed with flecks of blue. A tiny scar interrupted the sweep of one eyebrow. This close, her lips looked so much fuller.

Those lips moved now, quivering as Shelby managed a few hoarse words.

"Seems I'm still getting used to the traffic."

A second of inattention and she might have ended up in the hospital, or worse. Instead she was lying here, her back a foot off the ground, her mind spinning and nerve endings crackling with awareness.

This was a city where stories came to life. Right now she felt as if *she* were in a movie: a girl far from home almost demolished by a moment's distraction. Instead she'd been saved with the help of a tall, tawny-eyed man, who felt so hot and capable holding her in this tango-type dip that, if she weren't so dazed, she might well melt.

Dex carefully set her on her feet. As the numerous sounds and lights faded back up, Shelby schooled her expression, straightened her twisted dress and told her rabid pulse to quit pounding so wildly.

"You okay?" he asked.

"Everything except my pride," she admitted. "I feel stupid."

Judging from the curious looks of passersby, her incident was a bigger draw than Bernice's show.

"That paper that whipped out of your bag," he said. "It must've been important."

She remembered and her heart squeezed. "Sentimental value," she replied. Now that piece of her was gone forever.

Dex crossed to a nearby base-lit palm tree and swooped down. When he returned, the paper—a photo—was in his hand. Shelby's breath let out in a rush. Accepting it from him, she pressed the picture close for a second then placed it in her tote, in a zipped compartment this time.

"A person I respect very much," he said, "used to say that sentiment is never overrated."

While now didn't seem the right time to ask who that person might be, Shelby decided she'd like the opportunity to find out…maybe over a late dinner.

"Is that invitation to visit your scriptwriter still open?" she asked.

His face broke into a big white smile. "Rance and I would be honored."

A few minutes later, he was opening the passenger-side door of a sleek black Italian sports car. After she'd slipped into the leather bucket seat and buckled up, the engine growled to life and the pristine machine rolled into a break in the traffic.

"Does this sort of emergency script thing happen often?" she asked, trying not to double-guess this decision or feel overwhelmed. Far too much had happened today. She wouldn't be surprised if she woke up and found this had all been a dream.

"When you decide to make a movie," Dex said, changing up gears, "there are all kinds of challenges."

"I imagine a room filled with smoke," she said, "and a man sitting at the end of a long table, tapping away madly on a typewriter while someone else paces back and forth, head down, hands clasped behind his back."

Dex sent over a look.

"A typewriter?"

She reconsidered. "Guess that's a little last-century."

"They have heard of the internet where you come from, right?" he teased.

"Oh, sure. We put a cow on a treadmill to generate the extra electricity."

He laughed, and that warm deepwater feeling swirled around her again.

"I'm not a native to these parts, either," he offered. "I grew up in Australia."

"That explains the accent. I thought maybe British."

"We Aussies have better tans."

In the shadows, her gaze swept over his neck, his hands. From what she could see, he was naturally beautifully bronzed.

"Australia's halfway around the world," she said, forcing her gaze away from his classic profile—the strong jaw and hawkish nose. "What made you move here? Fame and fortune?"

Or had he run away from something? It happened.

"My family owns Hunter Enterprises."

"Which owns Hunter Productions, I presume." His movie company.

He clocked down a gear to take a bend. "My mother was born near your neck of the woods."

"Oklahoma?"

"Georgia, actually."

"Um, hate to tell you, but Georgia's nowhere near Oklahoma."

"Oh dear. I am still new to town, aren't I?"

Smiling, too, she settled more into her seat. "Back to your story…"

"My mother and father found each other at a Fox Theater event. Dad was taken with her Southern charm and beauty. He proposed the next month."

She grinned. "Your daddy's a romantic."

"He sure did love my mom." Dex's thoughtful smile faded. "When she died a few years back, he married again."

"A nice woman?"

"My father thinks so."

Heading down a less busy stretch of road, he stepped on the gas. With the engine growling and scenery slicing by, she waited for him to say more about his stepmom, but he didn't, which seemed to say a lot.

Soon they rolled into a wide private drive situated in an up-market neighborhood. A dark-haired man around her height answered the towering wood-paneled door. When he noticed her, the glare behind his trendy spectacles said he wasn't pleased.

Shelby thought about turning on her heel and finding her own way back to her apartment. Instead she found the wherewithal to appear unaffected. She'd dealt with and survived those kinds of looks before.

The moment passed, introductions were exchanged and Rance Loggins invited them both inside.

Dex and Rance traded a few words as they moved down a glass-walled corridor that showcased the tropical gardens outside. In a room decorated in hardwood, gleaming steel and slate-gray leather, Shelby quietly took a seat on a cloud-soft sofa while Dex shucked off his suit jacket and draped it over the back of a chair.

As he began going over the problem scene with Rance, Dex lowered himself down beside her—too close, Shelby thought, yet strangely not close enough. Whether having him save her from hitting the pavement earlier or the simple fact the other person in the room wasn't thrilled at his surprise company, she felt somehow safer knowing Dex was close. Safer and also hyperaware—of his scent. Of his heat.

His thigh was only a reach away, obviously muscled, long and strong. Her focus shifted to his polished big black shoes. Those feet sure would thump around in a pair of cowboy boots.

"So, what do you think?"

With a start, Shelby brought herself back to the conversation. Dex had spoken to her, and both he and Rance were waiting for a reply.

"What do I think about what?"

Rance reiterated the scenario—Shelby was sure more for his and Dex's benefit than hers.

"The female lead was the groom's girlfriend until he cheated on her. Broke her heart. Later he proposed to her friend. She's at the wedding reception and has bumped into her ex. Now they're standing face-to-face."

Dex thatched his fingers behind his head and stretched out those long trousered legs. "She needs to slap his face. Stomp his foot. Throw a drink in his face. We just need the words."

"I'm telling you," Rance said, "there's no surprise in that. The audience will expect it."

Shelby wet her lips, took a breath. She could see it all so clearly.

"She needs to speak up. She needs to speak to everyone there."

Dex lowered his hands and studied her. "You mean confront him in front of the entire reception crowd about his cheating?"

"She's classier than that," Shelby said. "She'd gather herself and, never feeling more alone, in her cucumber-soup-stained dress, with everyone knowing and pitying her, she'd ask for the microphone and say what a gorgeous couple the bride and groom make. How she wished them every happiness. When she hands back the mic, with tears glistening in her eyes, the audience won't applaud. As she walks away, weaving between tables then out wide arched doors that let in the sunshine, every guest is quiet. They've heard the rumors. In their hearts they already know. Reese and Kurt's relationship won't last."

"You mean Jada and Pete's relationship."

Shelby blinked across at Rance and gave a thin smile.

"Sure," she said. "That's who I mean."

Dex sat mesmerized. What just happened? Shelby had no experience with scripts or storytelling as far as he knew, and yet she'd enthralled them both with her rendition of how this pivotal scene ought to play out. Except…who were Kurt and Reese? And an even bigger question now was…behind that homegirl front, who was Shelby Scott?

Running a hand back through his shock of dark hair, Rance jumped up. "Let's get that down." He slipped in behind the laptop, pushing aside the hard copy, which was fanned out over the tabletop. "We'll need more backstory."

Three hours passed, during which Shelby joined Rance at the table, Chinese was ordered in and the scene ended up in great shape. On his fifth cup of coffee, Rance turned at enough of an angle to sling an elbow over the back of his chair.

"Do you write, Shelby?" he asked.

"Not my strength." Shaking back her mane of mahogany hair, she admitted, "But I watch a lot of movies."

Dex pushed away his empty box of chow mein. "Have an all-time favorite?"

"You'll laugh."

"Bet I won't."

"I like silent movies," she admitted. "I like Valentino."

"So do a lot of women in L.A." Rance stood and stretched his back. "The *haute couture* kind."

She laughed, and Dex saw Rance's face light in a way he'd never seen before. After a nasty bust-up, Rance hadn't dated in over a year. Dex guessed that tonight his friend had decided the drought should end.

"I don't have much interest in high fashion," she said.

"You should." Rance sauntered over to where she sat. "I'm sure high fashion would like *you*. The screen, too. I'm surprised Dex hasn't offered you a read."

"Of a movie role?" She set down her chopsticks. "I don't much like talking in front of people unless they're kids."

While she explained her nanny background and how tonight's meeting had come about, Dex mulled over her admission. He wasn't sold. She *had* spoken in front of a crowd at least once in her life, and the mysterious Reese and Kurt had comprised the subject matter.

As if she'd read his mind, her green gaze hooked over and caught his. Then she studied the time on her drugstore wristwatch and declared, "I need to get home."

"Beauty sleep?" Rance asked with a *you're beautiful enough* shine in his eyes.

"Shift starts at seven." She found her feet. She'd already explained her work as a waitress on The Strip.

"Shelby's place serves the best cheeseburgers in town," Dex said. "And the best coffee—when I can keep it in my cup."

He and Shelby shared a private smile before she began collecting empty boxes. "I'll clean up."

"You're my guest," Rance insisted.

"Neither of you would let me pay my share. This is my contribution."

"You've done enough with your help on that script," Dex pointed out.

"More than enough," Rance added.

But, her mind made up, Shelby had already gathered up the boxes.

When she was out of earshot in the kitchen, Rance readjusted his glasses.

"She's not your regular flavor. At first I thought she was another wannabe actress hoping to ride on your coattails all the way up to leading-lady heaven."

"And now?"

Rance held his heart. "I'm in love."

That was Dex's cue to laugh. But he didn't. Instead he stood and offered his friend a warning.

"She's off-limits."

"I thought she said you liked her for a babysitting gig?"

"And I don't need her distracted from her job."

"This is for your little brother, right? A vacation. Some time building sand castles. Couple days doing Disneyland. You're not signing Shelby to a five-year contract." He tapped finger-tips on top of his hard copy. "She might enjoy having a stab at a different kind of role."

"Helping you with scripts?"

"Why not?"

He'd tell him why not.

"She's young. A nice girl from a small town. She doesn't need anyone confusing issues."

"And I suppose you have no intention of throwing a few of your own complications in."

Dex was about to set Rance straight. Certainly Shelby was a beauty in all senses of the word, but he wasn't laying a trap for her. He didn't plan on seducing her, no matter how much he might like to.

Shelby reappeared.

"So, we're done here?" she asked.

Rance's grin was wry. "For the time being."

After goodbyes, Dex and Shelby were back on the road. He put the address she gave him into the GPS while mulling over Rance's comments. Shelby had been in town a second, and already she was attracting attention because of her looks and intelligence. Her modest brand of charm. As he pulled the car out and headed down the street, Dex decided that he'd need to get her signed before someone else snapped her up as a baby-sitter, model, actress, script doctor or, possibly, wife. Things happened fast in this town.

He tapped his thumbs on the steering wheel. "Rance thinks you're a natural."

"Beginner's luck."

"Or legitimate talent."

"You don't have to butter me up, Mr. Hunter."

"The name's Dex."

"Either way, I haven't changed my mind about working for you."

He frowned across at her. "You believe me about Bernice, don't you?" Gazing ahead, she nodded. "So what is it? You don't enjoy Chinese? I have a housekeeper, so no chores there. I'll get a cook in, too. Should have done it years ago." She remained silent. "Did I mention your own suite overlooking the ocean?"

She turned her head away.

He tried to keep the annoyance from his voice. "You're not giving me, or Tate, a chance."

But she simply continued to gaze out at the Los Angeles streets whirring by. Dex gripped the wheel tighter. Man, she was stubborn. He only wished she wasn't so darn attractive.

They arrived at Shelby's apartment block, a modest complex situated in a nice enough neighborhood. Nevertheless, he cut off the engine and swung open his door to see her in. Shelby was already out and on the pavement.

"You don't have to see me to the door," she said as he joined her.

"This isn't up for negotiation."

"You're right. It's not."

But when she headed off, he followed. His mother had raised her sons to see women home properly. That went for Miss Independence here, too, whether she liked it or not.

When he headed up the path and passed her, she took a moment; then, out of options, she continued on, as well. At the entrance's security door, however, she held her ground.

"Thank you for the evening. It was…different."

"Thank you for the help."

He was sure that when Rance returned from his week away, he would be checking out every café on The Strip to pass on his personal thanks, too.

Moving to key her code into the pad, she stopped to think and lowered her hand.

"I'm sorry I can't see my way clear to help with your brother. It's just…I think you'd do better with someone who's more familiar with how your kind of circles work."

"Shelby, I wouldn't want you for this job if you were from those circles. I need a responsible caretaker for a five-year-old when his big brother can't be around. I'm not after a hostess who can swing all the Hollywood ropes."

When he saw a glimmer of *maybe* in her eyes, he had an idea.

Finding his cell phone, he brought up a video. "I shot this when I flew out to Australia last."

Holding back a tumble of hair, she edged closer.

"That's Tate?" she asked.

"Mucking around in the surf at a Sydney beach."

With the summer sun at his back, Tate swayed as spent waves pushed up around his little legs then dragged back out to sea, almost sweeping him along, too. The tug finally brought him down onto his bottom. Splashing his hands in the wet sand, he giggled madly at the camera.

Shelby laughed, too, and when the video ended, she kept her gaze down. Eventually she hugged herself, then finally her head tilted and those incredible green eyes found his.

"He's real cute," she said.

"And smart. And loving. For a little kid, he gives the biggest bear hugs."

Her smile grew again before fading into a thoughtful look. "This is the place where all kinds of stories come to life. But I don't want to become a star, or even rub shoulders with the rich and famous. There's way more ordinary folk live here than highflyers, and I never thought past working for an average family with a couple everyday kids. But you're anything but average. When I'm with you, I have no idea what to expect next. I'm not a fan of surprises."

"Sometimes surprises are good."

She didn't seem convinced. "Do you intend to have company over while your brother's in your house?"

"If you mean women, I'm not seeing anyone. Even if I were, this is Tate's time."

Working his edge, he mentioned a salary figure and her eyes widened.

"Tate might not even like me," she said.

"Don't think we have to worry about that."

She thought some more.

"How long would you need me?"

"How does a six-month contract sound?"

She frowned. "His parents are okay with him being away that long?"

Dex hesitated. Shelby already thought his life was a whirlwind. No point revealing the more urgent reason behind Tate's visit just yet. Whoever had planned those assassination attempts on Guthrie's life had almost succeeded in kidnapping not only the Hunter patriarch but also his youngest son. Although the target had been Hunter Senior, never Tate, Guthrie wanted his baby boy well out of the way until this danger had passed. Unfortunately no one knew when that would be.

She wanted to know, why a six-month contract?

"I simply want to make it worth your while," Dex replied, which was true.

When, clearly torn, she gnawed her lip, he prodded.

"Come on, Shelby. Say yes, for Tate's sake."

"I'd want to keep this place for days off and, well, in case things don't work out."

"Of course."

After an eternity, she gave a small nod, then a smile. "Give me a start date and I'll be there."

He could have hugged her—and tight. Not a good idea. He'd be content with those few seconds he'd held her after that black sedan had nearly plowed her down. He was certain that kind of judgment glitch on her part wouldn't happen again. Too close of a call.

"Let's say Friday," he said.

"That soon?"

"Tate's here in a week. We need to get the place organized. Get provisions and equipment in."

"Oh. Sure." She drew her willowy frame up tall. "I can do that."

"Shall we shake on it?"

She took his extended hand, and that transfixing sensation he'd experienced when he'd caught her earlier seized him again. Pleasant. Heart pumping. Inappropriate. He'd got what he needed and now he should count himself lucky and go. And yet after this simple skin-on-skin contact, suddenly he really wanted to stay. But that would require her asking him inside, which would never happen. He didn't know her well, but she certainly wasn't the kind to invite in a man she'd known less than a day for a drink.

A delicious heat spread over Shelby's limbs, echoing in her chest, through to her core before she gathered herself and found the wherewithal to wind her hand away. Brushing her tingling palm down the side of her dress, she forced words past the thickness blocking her throat.

"I'll be in touch," she said.

"I look forward to it."

Over the noise of distant traffic and a TV blaring from some nearby window, Dex's voice sounded deeper. Gravelly and rich. Had he felt that amazing electric surge, too? The warmth had been so frighteningly tempting…enough to wonder if she ought to ask him to stay for a nightcap. Or wish she'd never met him at all.

She didn't want to feel attracted to any man, particularly a man like Dex Hunter. Obviously he liked women. Women would sure as beans like him. And she didn't want to get involved with anyone—not for any reason. Past experience was still too raw in her mind.

There was an awkward loaded moment where his lidded

gaze stayed fused to hers as if he were waiting for that invitation in. When she lifted her chin, his shoulders rolled back, he tipped his head and while she entered the building, he proceeded to his car.

A moment later, inside her partly furnished apartment, Shelby moved to the bedroom, sat on the edge of the mattress and, thinking back, drew out the decades-old photo that had been torn away on that sudden gust. Not so long ago, she had ripped it into pieces. Then, before leaving Mountain Ridge for good, she'd painstakingly taped the bits together again.

The girls in the photo seemed like ghosts to Shelby now. One had hair the color of a chestnut; the other's locks were as fair as a magnolia bloom. Friends since early grade school, they'd loved each other unreservedly. Had shared everything.

But some things were off-limits, even where best friends were concerned.

Three

As he headed home, Dex's thoughts were dragged away from Shelby Scott's ever-growing allure when his cell phone buzzed. He connected the call, and his younger brother Wynn's voice swelled out from the hands-free speaker. Frowning, Dex caught the time display on the dash.

"Bro, it's two in the morning in New York. What's up? Decide to get a head start on the morning's five-mile run?"

"I'm not that organized."

Really?

Wynn had his father's tenacity and his mother's heart. Unlike his older brothers, early on Wynn had decided he wanted to settle down and have a family. He wanted the *happily ever after* his parents had shared before their mother had passed away.

Maybe that's what this call was about, Dex thought now. Maybe on the heels of Cole's engagement news, Wynn had an announcement of his own. Absolutely made sense, given he and his photographer girlfriend, Heather Matthews, had been inseparable for over two years.

"Did you get Cole's message?" Dex asked. "Can't believe he's found the woman of his dreams. She must be something else to hold his attention away from the boardroom."

"Great news. I'm happy for him."

"No chance of you and Heather making it a double ceremony?"

"Heather and me... We're taking a break."

Dex almost swerved off the road. They'd seemed smitten whenever he saw them on family get-togethers back home in Sydney. Committed. Or Wynn had been, at least.

"Actually," Wynn went on, "it's pretty much over. We're still friends."

"God, Wynn... Man, I'm so sorry."

"It's late afternoon in Australia but Cole's not picking up. Any more news on Dad and his situation?"

Respecting Wynn's feelings—his need to move the conversation along—Dex got his thoughts together and summarized.

"Well, you know that after that first incident when his vehicle was run off the road, Dad was targeted again. Gunshot missed him by inches. Thankfully his P.I. was on hand when that maniac showed up a third time."

"He'd been visiting Uncle Talbot."

"Guess after all these years, Dad finally wants to mend fences."

Decades ago, Guthrie had assumed the chairmanship of Hunter's then much smaller family business, which had comprised print media only. Although he'd been assigned a position of authority, Guthrie's brother had felt marginalized, patronized. Eventually he'd walked out. The grudge festered into a long-standing feud.

Dex believed that break was part of the reason why, after Guthrie's heart surgery a few years back, he had divvied up Hunter Enterprises' now worldwide interests evenly among this generation of brothers. Wynn had been given rule over Hunter's print sector.

As far as Dex was concerned, Wynn had drawn the short

straw. Steering that side of the business through the digital revolution needed not only brains but also a steely nerve. In times such as these, profits could be made but long-standing empires could just as easily crumple.

If Wynn felt the pressure, he never complained or asked for help. Which, Dex deduced, might one day be his brother's professional undoing.

"After that shooting, Dad's P.I. chased the guy, right?" Wynn was saying. "Can't believe the fool ran straight into traffic."

"Apparently he'd had a beef with the Broadcasting News Division," Dex said, easing onto the freeway that would see him home in five. "When he didn't regain consciousness, that should have been the end of it."

But the worst was yet to come. Wynn also knew that, not long after the incident outside Uncle Talbot's, their father had been assaulted in broad daylight. Dex's stomach muscles clutched remembering how close Guthrie and Tate had come to being shoved into that black van something like a week after the shooting incident, perhaps never to be seen or heard from again. He'd give his eyeteeth to know who and what was behind it all.

"Tate's coming out here for a visit," Dex told Wynn. "Dad wants him out of the way in case there's more trouble. He wanted his wife, Eloise, to vacate Sydney, too, but in her third trimester, she's staying put."

"Guess she wants to be with her husband."

Dex couldn't contain it. "You and your rose-colored glasses."

"We might not approve of his marriage, but we should support it."

Dex wondered if Wynn even suspected. Last Christmas Eve, when the family was all together under one roof, Dex had interrupted their dear stepmom trying to play pucker-up with a repulsed Cole. Dex's older brother had thundered out of the room while Eloise tittered on to Dex about having a lash in her eye. Quite a piece of work.

He'd been torn for a time, as Cole must have been. No one

wanted to see someone they loved be made to look like a fool. But neither did a son want to cause trouble in his father's marriage. When these attempts had begun on their father's life, Cole had admitted he'd suspected Eloise. Private checks had cleared her of involvement—on that score at least.

Wynn said he'd keep in touch and ended the call at the same time Dex pulled into his garage. As he exited the car and passed through the internal door leading to the kitchen, he shook his head over the torment his father had endured. Some deranged people imagined they had the right to intimidate others. Some felt compelled to hurt—financially, emotionally. Physically.

On his way through to the living room, Dex lifted his nose and frowned. Smoke? A movement outside, beyond glass sliders, caught his eye. Something on the back lawn, no more than a foot high, was glowing red. He edged over, slid open the door and moved outside.

Positioned before the palm-fringed pool, a box that resembled a crude miniature coffin stood smoldering. When a piece fell to the grass, sparks spat out. A couple hit his trouser leg but, while a chill ran up his spine, Dex didn't move to slap them away. This message was patently clear.

Recently he'd received a threatening letter; if he didn't pay, an unfortunate incident years back would come to light. He knew that the incident to which the letter referred involved his friend Joel and an industrial building burning down. Thankfully the building had been empty at the time. That didn't excuse the act. Arson was a criminal offense. So too was withholding evidence.

Although Dex had mentioned the note to Cole, he hadn't taken the threat seriously. But now he wondered. Could this somehow be connected to his father's trouble? Was the scum involved with his father's assassination attempts for some reason widening his net?

Either way, how could he bring Tate here now?

Four

"Can't you *please* take me with you when you go?"

Shelby stopped wiping a tabletop to smile over at her friend and fellow waitress.

"It's not so bad here," she told Lila Sommers. "Besides, you'll hear about your college application soon and, in no time, you'll be way ahead of the game." Shelby sighed. "A double degree. I can't imagine how full of brains your head must be."

"I'm not so bright that I can land a job with one of this town's most eligible bachelors. Dex Hunter's been coming here ordering cheeseburgers and fries forever."

"I'm not sure about your interpretation of eligible. Being single doesn't necessarily make someone the pick of the bunch."

"Okay." Lila began counting fingers. "Let's move onto charismatic. Absurdly handsome. Dripping with money."

"Which you know has nothing to do with why I took the job."

This morning while they'd set up, Shelby had filled Lila in on the previous night, ending with how she'd made the mistake of looking at that video featuring Dex's little brother. Until then she'd decided she wasn't a good fit with his world. From jumping to conclusions over Bernice and that unfortunate embrace, to nearly falling in front of a vehicle, then being invited to a genuine movie script session…

Merely being in his orbit left her feeling gauche.

But, irrespective of her pedestrian style—or, as Dex had said, *because* of it—he wanted her to be his brother's temporary nanny. Watching Tate play around in the surf, seeing that exuberant expression light his little face… She couldn't help but want to give Tate the stability he deserved when he came out to visit his high-flying older brother. She also wanted to hear that gorgeous giggle again.

"You must want a batch of your own someday?" Lila asked, straightening salt and pepper shakers, pushing in chairs.

Children of her own? She'd love that more than anything. But she pointed out, "I have to find the right guy first."

And, for the time being, she wasn't looking.

"You never know. Dex Hunter might be that man."

"Didn't your mama ever tell you? It's the charmers you need to watch out for."

"My mom's middle name is Man-Hater. Her advice is to stay away, period."

"Guess she's been burned."

"Big-time—by my dad."

"Oh, Lila, I'm sorry."

"It's between them." Lila straightened her apron then flicked back her brunette ponytail. "Dad and I are cool. Now that he knows how much I want to do college, he says he'll help pay my tuition." She went to wipe the next table. "If I get in."

Shelby thought of her own father, an anchor, a safe guiding light.

"I don't hate men," she said. "But I am steering clear for a while."

"I wouldn't have thought so the way you were looking at Dex yesterday. Nothing to be ashamed of. If a guy like him showed me that kind of interest, I'd melt like milk chocolate on a grill."

Heat suffusing her cheeks, Shelby pushed in a final chair. "There's work to do. Lunch rush'll be pouring in soon."

"Wouldn't it be a fairy tale come true if you two fell in love, got engaged—"

Shelby snapped out her cloth. "No fairy tale happening here." Given that she'd confided in her friend about that embarrassing predicament back home, Lila ought to know she wasn't thinking that way. Or shouldn't be. "I'll work for Dex Hunter on a purely professional basis or I won't work for him at all."

"Great we got that all cleared up."

At the sound of that amused, masculine voice and the sudden stunned look on Lila's face, Shelby held her breath and slowly turned around. Dressed in jeans and a casual button-down, Dex stood before her, a teasing smile slanting his lips. He looked so laid-back, weight on one leg, shoulders angled, and yet those tawny eyes held that same intensity…the same knowledge and hunger that had left her legs feeling as wobbly as Jell-O last night when they'd parted.

None of that changed the fact she'd meant what she'd said. She wasn't interested in romance. She wasn't concerned about his broad, hard chest, his palpable sex appeal…that entrancing bone-melting smile.

Shelby mentally shook herself. What was he doing here anyway?

"What's wrong?" she asked. "You're perspiring." Beads of sweat were glistening high on his brow.

"It's a hot day." He wound his already folded cuffs up another turn as if to prove it. "I just dropped by to say there's been a change of plans."

"Tate's not coming?"

Mother hen Lila stepped in. "You do realize she's resigned. The boss kicked the wall and said she could leave now except he'd be short for the lunch rush."

"Tate's still coming out," Dex assured them both. "In fact, he'll be here late tomorrow."

"Last night you said a week."

Dex folded into a chair. "I phoned Sydney this morning to… arrange some things. Cole, the brother stationed in Australia, is set to leave on a sabbatical. He wanted Tate's trip signed and sealed before he left. My father agreed."

"Suddenly you don't look so happy about it."

"I had some other news last night," Dex explained as Lila laid a coffee before him then hung around to wipe an already sparkling table. "I need other accommodations until a minor problem's sorted at my place."

"Problem as in plumbing or a hole in the roof?"

"More like rodents in the basement." His pensive gaze flicked up from his steaming cup. "I've organized a suite in town. I'd like you to help me get the place organized."

One minute she was a waitress, next she was being whisked away to a hotel by a multimillionaire. She had to catch her breath. Shelby slid into the seat beside him.

Behind them, her boss's unhappy voice ground out.

"Those chairs are for patrons only."

Shelby jumped up. Mr. Connor's usually nonexistent jaw was jutting. On either side of a bulbous nose, his small dark eyes narrowed. He addressed his remarks to Dex.

"She's here to serve tables. You're a good customer, but I have a business to run."

Dex got to his feet. "Shelby was taking my order."

Connor exhaled as if he'd heard it all before. "Look, we don't run that kind of establishment. If you want to—you know— *chat,* there are other places for that."

Shelby's temper flared. Did Connor call her what she thought he'd just called her? She stuck out her own chin.

"Now wait a minute—"

Dex held up a hand. "Let me handle this." He addressed Connor. "Obviously that isn't the kind of discussion I'm having with Ms. Scott."

"It looked pretty cozy to me," Connor replied. "Particularly after your nice long talk yesterday." He eyed Shelby. "Don't think I didn't notice."

"I've offered Shelby employment," Dex said. "I believe she passed on her resignation to you this morning."

"So it was you." Connor narrowed his gaze again. "Sure. She resigned, but I still have her till the end of the week."

"I was hoping," Dex continued, "that you might consider releasing her earlier than that."

"Like when?"

"Like now."

Connor shrugged. "Like I said, I have a business to run."

Dex drew out his wallet. "I'm sure we can come to some arrangement—"

"I don't want your money."

Dex scratched his temple. "We need to settle this somehow…" He peeled off a few big bills.

Connor sniffed, then put out his palm. "Fine. But I'll warn you. She's not worth it."

While Dex's expression darkened, Shelby shrank back. She might want to deck Connor, but she suspected Dex just might do it. But then a crooked smile eased up one corner of Dex's mouth and he stuffed the notes down the front of Mr. Connor's Hawaiian-print shirt.

"That amount should cover any inconvenience or losses to your establishment. Now, I'm sure we'd all prefer that this parting be amicable." His voice dropped and hardened. "Doesn't have to be." He peeled off another couple bills and offered them to Lila. "Thanks for the impeccable service in the past. I've enjoyed the food, even if your boss is a jerk."

He asked Shelby to get her handbag. It took her ten seconds. When she was back, he grabbed her hand. She kept up as he headed out of the shop and down the busy sidewalk.

"Connor's face was blotched, he was so mad," she said.

"Connor's an oaf."

"Do you usually give oafs huge amounts of money to shut them up?"

"No, I don't. But it was either that or shut him up another way." Connor was lucky he hadn't collected a broken jaw. Dex dragged a palm across his growling stomach and winced. "Damn, I'm hungry."

"You get hungry when you're mad?"

Usually he didn't get angry.

"Must be some primitive instinct to refuel before and after battle, I guess."

"When I want to let go and punch something," she said as they strode past people strolling on either side of them, "I jump on my horse and take a long hard ride."

"Not as good as knocking back a stack of pancakes."

"Much better for the waistline."

He paused and glanced at her. She looked hotter in that uniform than he remembered. Even in a burlap bag, Shelby's assortment of curves would be difficult to dismiss. Pretty much impossible to forget. Her waistline had nothing to worry about.

Their stride had slowed. And he was still holding her hand. Clearing his throat, he let go.

"Have you hired an exterminator for the rodents?" she asked, shaking out her fingers. He must have been holding them tight.

"I'm not sure which method to take. Bait or blast."

"Sounds nasty."

"Nothing you or Tate will ever need to worry about." He rubbed his hands together. "Now let's get organized. We'll make a list. Groceries can be delivered to the suite."

"I'll personally choose any food to be prepared. You have to keep a close eye on what kids eat."

"I'm sure the delivery service has that covered."

"But I like to walk up and down the aisles."

He scratched his head. "Why?"

"I won't know everything I need until I see it."

Sounded like a lot of work to him, but her mind seemed

set so they found a market and gathered up staples—bread, eggs, meat, Oreos. And fresh vegetables, including spinach. Shelby insisted greens were important for a growing boy. So long as she didn't expect *him* to put any of that Popeye food near his plate.

Later, they arrived at the Beverly Hills Hotel. After porters collected the groceries, the valet parked the car and Dex checked in. They arrived at their suite at the same time as the porters. In the kitchen a moment later, he opened the first grocery bag and shuddered.

Shelby craned to see. "The way you screw up your nose around spinach, anyone would think it was covered in slime."

"That's exactly what it's like when it's cooked."

"It's packed full of vitamins."

"You sound like an advertisement."

She drew out a bag of carrots with the green bits still attached. "These are great for adding fiber to your diet. Vitamin A, too."

"I'm more your potato-done-any-way kind of man. I've never met a curly fry I didn't like."

A stack of cans in hand, she twirled around, found the pantry and headed over. "I make my own brand of fries. Hopefully you won't have to worry about feeding them to the dog under the table."

"I don't have a dog and you don't have to cook."

"Not even my specialty? Inch-thick seared juicy steak?"

He held his empty stomach. "You dare to talk that way when you know my condition?" He picked up a carton of cream. "Where are you on desserts?"

"I believe every day should end with wrapping your lips around something satisfyingly sweet."

His gaze dipped to her hips. Well, they were in agreement there.

She turned away from the pantry while he was on his way to the fridge, and they bumped into each other. He wound a steadying arm around her. The contact was harmless; she even laughed when he said, "We'll have to stop meeting like this." But he was acutely aware of his blood pumping way faster than it should. Of her breasts accidentally brushing his chest.

Moving apart, they each continued with their task.

"I forgot to say that your friend found me at the café this morning," she said. "He stopped by before heading out of town."

Wondering where to put the cured salami sausage, Dex frowned across at her. "You mean Rance?"

"He asked if I wanted a job as his assistant." She picked up a tub of butter. "I was flattered."

"But you didn't accept."

"I could be wrong but I think Mr. Loggins wants more in an assistant than I'm prepared to give. I even told him that. He didn't really answer, except to smile."

It wasn't hard to see that Rance was smitten. Although Dex would concede: Shelby did show promise as a script doctor.

She put the carton away in the fridge then found his gaze again.

"If I ask you something," she began, "will you tell me the truth?"

"Sure."

"You don't really have rats in your basement, do you?" When he hesitated, she qualified. "Long skinny tails. Hunched furry bodies. Tiny white fangs."

Leaning back against the opposite counter, Dex crossed his arms. Last night he'd wondered if the threats he'd received might somehow be linked to his father's trouble. But he'd soon reverted to his earlier conclusion. The situations were unrelated. Whoever lay behind these extortion attempts was a coward. A lowlife who, Dex believed, didn't have the guts to confront him face-to-face.

He wished he could turn back time. Change things.

Three years ago, his friend Joel Chase had broken down and sworn that, while he'd gone to that building with revenge on his mind, at the eleventh hour he'd had a change of heart. Unfortunately, rather than blow out the lit match, he had fumbled. The accelerant had done the rest. Dex had never been so torn in his life. How many others found themselves in that kind of predicament? Given no one was hurt, and Joel had been filled with remorse, he'd kept his mouth shut. Now, as then, Joel had way more to lose than Dex if the truth ever got out.

But this storm would pass. It must, because Dex would pirouette in public dressed in nothing but a pink tutu before handing over blackmail money to anyone for any reason. If Tate wasn't coming to visit, Dex would have stayed put, laid a trap and confronted the creep if he dared to pull any more sick pranks. For now it was enough that he'd had those surveillance cameras hooked up.

He answered Shelby's question about rats. "Let's just say I needed to get out of that place for a while."

"If there's something you should tell me," Shelby pushed, "best tell me now."

"There's nothing for you to worry about."

"I have this prickly feeling running up my back, and I've learned to listen when that happens."

"There was a time when you didn't listen?"

She blinked, recovered, then found a container of coffee. "We're not talking about me."

As she put the coffee away, Dex unraveled his arms. He hadn't meant to spook her, but now he hoped she'd let those other questions drop. Although, frankly, he'd still like some answers about *her* past. Did her earlier prickling feelings involve Reese and Kurt?

She crunched up the last empty grocery bag and dropped it in the trash. "Done and finished."

He pushed off the counter. "Let's check out the place."

The living space was roomy. White walls and carpet—probably unwise with a young boy crashing around the place. Facing the plasma screen TV and elevated view of the palm-lined pool and cabanas, the U-shaped dark leather sofa was huge.

He read Shelby's face. *Comfortable. Low-maintenance.* She moved to the glass doors.

"Can we have the outdoor table and chairs put away somewhere?" she asked.

A good safety measure for curious kids who could climb like monkeys.

"Consider it done," he said.

She turned to face him and, with the afternoon sun slanting in, her hair looked as if it were threaded with strands of shining copper.

"Why did you choose a suite in a hotel rather than a house?" she asked.

He dragged his gaze away from her glowing silhouette to concentrate. "Tate'll have everything he needs. A pool and swings and a big playroom." And first-class security. He studied the giant plasma. "We'll need games and controls."

"I'd prefer games we can play together. Books, paints and blocks, too."

His chest grew warm at a memory…he and Cole and their mom building wobbling towers that more often than not tumbled down before they were finished. Then they'd sigh—or clap and laugh—and do it all again.

"You're old-fashioned," he said.

"It's called being involved."

"Are you?"

Perplexed, she laughed. "Of course. I get involved with any child I care for."

Actually he'd meant romantically involved and, although she avoided commenting more by going to check out the playroom situation, he suspected that she knew it.

Five

Two days later at an LAX arrivals gate, Shelby's heart almost burst watching Dex sweep his cute-as-a-button brother up into the air and swirl him around.

"How was the flight?" he asked an excited Tate, whose face was split with a grin. "Were the crew good to you?"

"Daddy got a special lady to sit by me the whole way." Tate waggled a finger toward the stream of passengers pouring out from the gate. "That's her."

A woman sauntered over. She was of average height but that was as far as average went. Her thick ash-blond hair was drawn into a luxurious ponytail that flowed over one shoulder and down to her waist. Her eyes were big, widely spaced and a startling ice-blue. Toned arms and lithe build said keeping in shape was her lifestyle of choice. But that aura of confidence was her best quality. Proud and assured, she might have owned the world and would just as happily have given it away.

Meanwhile, Dex looked blindsided. "No one told me…"

Coming closer, the woman threw up her hands. "We wanted to surprise you, you big dope."

Tate held his stomach; he was giggling that hard. "Your mouth dropped all the way down," he told Dex and then showed him a five-year-old's interpretation of stunned—eyes crossed, tongue out.

Growling playfully, Dex gave the woman a huge hug. "What are you doing here?"

"I flew out to Sydney to see how Dad was doing," the woman—Dex's sister?—said. "Dad was stressing about getting Tate over here with you as soon as possible. So we pushed it all forward, I volunteered to chaperone and here we are."

Shelby digested it all…but couldn't figure out why Guthrie Hunter should be so anxious about organizing his youngest son's visit to L.A. This was just a vacation, right?

Bouncing Tate up onto his hip, Dex remembered introductions. "Teagan, meet Shelby."

Shelby smiled, nodded. "Shelby Scott."

"Shelby's new to town," Dex said. "She's offered to help me look after this little guy while he's here visiting."

While Dex ruffled his brother's hair, Shelby stepped closer to say hello. His eyes were the same unusual tawny color as Dex's but without the flashes of blue.

"Your brother showed me a video of you splashing around in some waves," she said.

"I love the beach," Tate told her. "I'm a nipper now."

"A junior lifesaver?" Dex held up his hand for a high five. "Way to go!"

Teagan asked, "So how long have you two been dating?"

"No, no," Shelby said at the same time Dex hurried to explain. "I've employed Shelby to be Tate's nanny."

"Oh. I just assumed…" Teagan's quizzical expression evaporated on a big smile. "Well, it's great to meet you."

They collected luggage then strolled out to the parking lot with Tate chattering about dinosaurs and airplanes the whole way. Needing more seats than a sports car allowed, Dex had hired a luxury SUV. As he buckled Tate in, then piled bags in the back, Teagan spoke in Shelby's ear.

"Sorry about that misunderstanding. But it's not a leap that you two could be an item. If you weren't so glamorous and tall and beautiful—"

"Me? Glamorous?" In a plain cotton dress and no makeup? In any dress, for that matter.

"Well, you might be a nanny now, but I'd bet good money, if you stay in L.A., some lucky talent scout will snap you up." Teagan wound the sturdy black knapsack off her back. "My tip is to get a good agent, pronto."

"But I don't want to be snapped up."

"You don't have any aspirations to be a leading lady, earn squillions of dollars, be adored and watched by crowds?"

Shelby shuddered. "I'm not a fan of crowds."

Teagan looked shocked and pleased at the same time.

Settling Tate in the backseat, Dex called out, "Hey, you two can chat in the car. We need to get this boy home. He's got to be hungry."

Tate began chanting, "Cheeseburber, cheeseburber!"

While Teagan slid into the front passenger's seat, Shelby slipped in behind the driver's scat.

"Dex and I went shopping yesterday," Shelby let Tate know. "There are all kinds of great things to eat and do at home."

"I love your shack by the sea," Teagan said, belting up. "All three stories of it."

"Actually, we're staying at a hotel." Dex named the establishment and Teagan let loose a low whistle.

"You always did like the best. But you couldn't have sold your place. You bragged to everyone who'd listen about that view."

"This address is only temporary." Dex ignited the engine. "Everyone buckled up? Let's get this show on the road."

Shelby saw the same questions in Teagan's eyes now that she'd wanted to ask when she'd learned about Dex's sudden move. But as long as the temporary change of address didn't concern her or Tate while he was here, what did it matter where he lived?

"Guess you want an update on Dad," Teagan said when they were on their way.

Tate was getting comfortable in his booster seat. "The bump on his head's all better now."

"That's real good, buddy," Dex replied then told Shelby, "Teagan runs her own fitness studio in Seattle."

Shelby remembered the woman's glowing complexion and bouncy step. "You don't work for the family business, Teagan?"

Dex reached over to squeeze his sister's shoulder. "She's our resident rebel, aren't you?"

"Translation," Teagan said, trying not to laugh as she shoved her brother's tickling grasp away while she pinned him with a mock stern look. "I wanted to make it on my own."

"Admirable," Shelby said.

"And necessary to my sanity."

Dex started another thread of conversation, although Shelby somehow thought the two were related.

"So you caught up with Cole while you were visiting," he said.

"I was pleasantly surprised." Teagan filled Shelby in. "You'd have to know our big brother to understand when I say he's a giant control freak, to the point of driving everyone up the wall. But that seems to have changed since he realized there are more important things in life than telling people what to do."

"Sounds like you might reconsider working for the business," Dex slipped in.

Teagan pretended not to hear. "His fiancée, Taryn Quinn, is a honey. Strong-willed, smart. Cole's match in every way. I never thought I'd say it but there's a side to Cole that's pure pussycat."

"I'm looking forward to the ceremony," Dex said with a grin in his voice.

"You're not married, Shelby?" Teagan asked.

"No." Shelby's hands flexed and bunched on her thighs. "Not married."

"Your accent...Texan?"

Dex replied for her. "Shelby comes from a little known place called Mountain Ridge, Oklahoma."

"Sounds so peaceful," Teagan said. "*Horse Whisperer* country."

She thought that was set in Montana but Shelby shrugged and confirmed, "We own a ranch."

"You like that life?"

"Very much."

Teagan looked back over her shoulder. "If you weren't chasing the limelight, what made you make the move to L.A.?"

Shelby felt Dex's curiosity, too. While her pulse rate jumped, she assumed a calm expression. "Well, you see—" she rubbed her suddenly damp palms down her skirt "—it was time I saw more of the world."

"Sounds like California's just the beginning then." Teagan moved around in her seat to face her. "I have a friend, a teacher. She flew overseas a couple years ago. Landed a job as a governess in France. She lives in a castle now. Can you believe it!"

"Stop giving her ideas," Dex growled, turning onto the highway. "I'd like to keep Shelby with me a while."

Studying the back of his head above the rest, seeing the smile creasing the corners of his eyes in the rearview mirror, Shelby felt the tension locking her shoulder blades ease. He sounded so determined. So sincere. And now that Tate was here and he seemed so happy and well-adjusted...

For the first time since seeing Dex being kissed by that poor woman that night, Shelby felt truly confident about agreeing to his terms.

"Can I please have annava cupcake before I go to bed?"

Dex, Shelby and special guests Teagan and Tate were all settled in the living room of his Beverly Hills Hotel suite. Despite his assertion that she didn't have to cook, Shelby had whipped up a magnificent roast with all the trimmings for dinner. She'd also baked scrumptious cupcakes—and not from a packet. Dex had very nearly asked to lick the bowl.

Now at Tate's understandable request, Dex sat straighter in his corner of the giant horseshoe-shaped sofa and mentally rubbed his hands together. Another cupcake? Great idea.

"Honey, you've already brushed your teeth," Shelby explained to Tate as she fanned out children's books on the coffee table.

"And those cakes were huge." Teagan set down her empty cup of herbal tea that smelled like brewed lawn clippings. Probably tasted like that, too. "One cake is plenty for a kid your size. And before you say anything, brother dear, you've already had four."

Appalled, Dex sat back. "Did not." He'd had three.

"You've always been driven by your taste buds." Teagan nodded at her brother's middle. "You'd better watch out or you'll look like a pear before you know it. I can set you up with a routine. Thirty minutes every day is all it takes to keep in shape."

Dex spoke to Shelby, a magnificent cook who would surely understand. "My sister doesn't appreciate a universal truth. Enjoying fine food is one of life's great pleasures."

"You should have been a chef," Teagan said. "Or a restaurant critic."

"Or I could open my very own place," Dex said, expanding on the idea. "And have my own blow-your-mind signature dessert."

"I can see it now." Teagan's palms drew fanfare arcs through the air. *"Sexy Dexy's Diner."*

"So informal." Dex grinned. "I like it! But watch your language in front of the boy." He swung a glance around. "Where'd he go?"

Teagan spotted Tate sneaking off to the kitchen, aka Magical Cupcake Land. She ran to grab him. "Not on my watch, sonny boy."

Dex muttered, "Talk about tough love."

"I think someone needs to hit the sack," Teagan said as

she led a yawning, bathed and pajamaed Tate back from the kitchen.

"After that big plane ride," Shelby said, "you must be tired."

Tate used fingers and a thumb to pry open one eye. "Am not."

Dex chuckled. Darn that kid was cute. When he had children—someday in the far distant, really remote future—he only hoped they were as perfect as Tate. "Buddy, we have weeks ahead of us."

"Lots of time," Teagan said to Tate before she murmured to Dex under her breath, "Just hope the *p-o-l-i-c-e* catch that guy soon."

Dex flicked Shelby a look. Her brow was creased as if she wasn't sure what to make of that remark. *Very subtle, sis. Not.* At least for Tate's sake she'd spelled out that giveaway word.

Dex had thought about tugging Teagan aside with a warning not to mention the stalker business unfolding in Australia. But Tate could just as easily mention the incident he'd been involved in recently and the fact the authorities were dropping by the Hunter mansion in Sydney with much regularity. That cat was bound to wiggle out of its bag one way or another.

"Tate, honey, what say I tuck you into bed?" Shelby leaned forward to scan the titles laid out on the table. "Look at all these amazing stories. There's a couple from your favorite series. We can read one together."

Tate hugged his big sister's leg. "I want Tea to tuck me in."

Shelby found the other woman's gaze. Teagan silently asked the designated caretaker, *That okay?* Shelby's smile said, *It's fine. Go ahead.*

Teagan got down on Tate's level. "There are two beds in your room and I'm pretty sure one has my name on it."

"Really? Wow! Show me."

"Kiss your brother and Shelby good-night first."

Tate trundled over and gave Dex a hug, little arms around his bruiser of a neck. Drawing back, Tate eyed Shelby and sucked in his bottom lip.

"That's okay." Shelby sent him a wink. "I'm shy about that kind of stuff, too. I'll see you tomorrow."

Tate took his big sister's hand. Together they disappeared behind the door of a bedroom that was decorated with matching racing car bedspreads, which Shelby had chosen earlier that day.

Shelby gazed down the corridor for a long moment before exhaling and gathering herself. "I'll go see to the dishes."

"They'll wait till morning."

"I'd rather do them now."

"In the morning."

"Now."

He frowned. "You're stubborn."

"Am not."

Which made him think of Tate's cute response to being tired. Shelby must have thought of him trying to keep his eyes open, too, because they both grinned. Eventually she relaxed and reclined back into the sofa while Dex snatched up a book.

"Kuddles Goes to Visit."

She tipped closer to study the front cover's illustration of a young koala perched in the fork of a gum tree. "Thought it'd be familiar for him."

"And Tate'll like it just as well tomorrow night."

"It's only natural he would want to be with his sister. I like her, too."

He slid the book back onto the tabletop. "Can't believe it's been four years since she flew the coop."

"Does Teagan get along with your stepmom?"

"Better than me and Cole, which isn't saying much."

"I swear Eloise Hunter must have a long nose with a wart. Does she seduce unsuspecting children into eating poisoned apples?"

"No wart. And in this story, the children are fully grown."

"You mean she tried to hurt you and your brother?"

"Eloise isn't much older than Cole. I have it on good authority the opposite sex finds him attractive."

"And?"

"And I don't want to give you the wrong idea about the home Tate's growing up in."

"Okay. Now I'm worried."

Dex rubbed his temple. Wasn't often words failed him, but this was a touchy subject.

"Eloise is drawn to powerful men," he said. "Scruples need not apply."

Realization then disgust flittered over her eyes. "She tried to come on to Cole? Her stepson?"

"She's pampered and bored—"

"And trying to seduce members of her own family. I can't even imagine…" Shelby shuddered. "What about the guy Teagan was talking about? The one she hoped police would catch?"

Dex surrendered the details surrounding the recent attempts on his father's life, including the day Hunter senior and Tate had almost been abducted and his father's head had been knocked, causing the bump the little boy had mentioned earlier.

"A passerby intervened. Thank God, or they'd both have been shoved in that van and…" He growled out a breath. "Well, who knows what would've come next. That's why Tate's here now for an indefinite amount of time."

"So he's out of harm's way. But why didn't you tell me?"

"I was waiting for the right time."

"You can't put off something as important as that."

"No one is in danger here."

"You hope."

He made himself clear. "That situation is all the way back in Australia. And it concerns my father, not Tate. He was simply in the wrong place at the wrong time."

Her gaze sharpened. "So all that has nothing to do with the rats in your basement?"

"Definitely not."

She scrutinized his face. But something in his expression must have confirmed he'd told her the truth. The two situations were unrelated. His blackmail threats were annoying, inconvenient, but nowhere near life-threatening.

While she mulled all that over, Dex checked in on Tate's bedroom.

"They're both out to it," he said, resuming his seat a moment later. "Teagan's snoring. She's done it her whole life. When she was fourteen, I recorded a particularly robust session. Sounded like a train in a tunnel. I played it back at the breakfast table the next morning."

"I hope she belted you."

"Dumped a bowl of cold milk in my lap. Mom told me to clean it up then apologize." His brow lowered. "You women like to stick together."

She gave him a wide smile. "And you never teased her again."

"She on the other hand derived some sick kind of pleasure from hiding frogs in my football boots."

"Oh, no!" She clapped a hand over her mouth but the laugh escaped. "Frogs?"

"Lucky none were squashed." At the end of his jeans, ten bare toes wiggled. "I have big feet."

"I noticed."

While he'd never thought Teagan's pranks funny back then, now—with Shelby openly laughing—he wished he could go back and live all those innocent moments again. All four kids had been so close. Then things had changed. A little like the moment was changing here and now.

As Shelby's laughter faded, easy smiles sobered and they were left looking into each other's eyes.

And Shelby had beautiful eyes.

When he'd returned from checking on Tate, he'd unwittingly sat a fraction closer to her. His leg nearest hers was hooked up so that the knee of his jeans rested lightly against the outside of her thigh.

"I think this is going to work out fine," he said.

Her gaze shuttered, lowered then found his again. "I should probably get to bed."

"It's been a long day for us all."

"A nice day."

He thought so, too.

"If you need help with anything going forward…" He allowed his focus to drop to her lips, for a heartbeat's slide around her cheek. "I mean, if you need help taste-testing new cupcake recipes…"

Her eyes sparkled again. "If you can suggest something better than my cookies 'n' cream mix."

He placed his arm along the back of the sofa and, bending his elbow, rested his cheek on a bed of knuckles. "I might have a few ideas."

"Something new and wild or more your traditional fare?"

"As long as the icing is sweet and the center light and moist."

"So, suggestions?"

He lowered his arm until its length lay along the back of the sofa and partly behind her. "Well, with regard to combining ingredients, I've discovered you need to fold in the right amounts at the right time."

"I see." Her lips twitched. "Any advice on heat?"

"It needs to build until it's high and constant."

"And the end product, I suppose, is—"

"Guaranteed to melt in your mouth."

The temptation was too great. He leaned in and when his lips feathered over hers, an electric bolt ripped through his body. She trembled as if she'd felt it, too. Then her eyes drifted shut and the impulse to trace his lips over hers again took a mighty hold. He tilted his head farther.

At the same time her eyes opened again and a smooth hand slid up between them, cordoning him off.

"You sound like quite the expert." Her voice was smoky as well as resigned. "But I'm afraid I don't let anyone near my kitchen."

His thumping pulse stumbled over a beat. He took in her words and frowned. "No one?"

She shimmied away from him. "I'm not here for this."

"I know, but—"

"I mean, don't you have enough notches on your bedpost?"

"Shelby, this has nothing to do with bedposts."

"What if your brother had wandered out here a moment ago?" In full charge of her faculties again, she combed two sets of fingers over her tumble of hair and glanced down the corridor to check. "He's just lived through one terrible ordeal."

"I wouldn't call this terrible—"

"And if you've seen his mother propositioning a man other than his father, maybe poor Tate has, too. He doesn't need to see adults making out on the couch. People he should be able to trust."

That pulled him up short.

He hadn't set out for this to happen, but truth was he wanted to kiss Shelby. Hell, he wanted to pull her clothes off and make wild crazy love to her till dawn. She was bright and funny and her smile made him want to do cartwheels. *And* she could cook. Boy, could she cook. Why in the name of everything sacred *wouldn't* he be attracted to her?

But she'd just poured a bucket of cold milk on his lap.

He was out of line. She was his employee. He wouldn't dream of seducing his female assistants or support staff at the studio. He was a healthy, inquisitive, high-functioning male but there were boundaries and he'd overstepped this one.

She'd made an even bigger point. Repositioned thousands of miles from home, Tate had recently survived an abduction attempt. His older brother should never put him in a position of possibly witnessing anything he might find confusing, upsetting.

Dex held his frown.

What was I thinking?

"You're right," he told her. About everything. He pushed to his feet. "I'm going to stand under a cold shower for ten minutes then I'm going to bed." By himself. "And don't worry. You have my word. While you're here, I swear I won't touch you again."

Six

Two days later, the four of them did Disneyland. The rides, the food, the sore feet—although, unlike the adults who were feeling it by the afternoon, Tate ran on high the entire time. Dex had never seen his little brother look so jazzed. Watching him jump around, his eyes so big with awe, had Dex thinking again about an inevitable stage in his life.

Kids of his own.

But he was still young. Only thirty. There was plenty of time to worry about being pinned down with those kinds of responsibilities…even if they turned out to be as adorable as this little guy, who didn't appear to have a care in the world.

Then disaster struck.

"You're leaving me, Tea?" Tate asked over the screams echoing from the scariest roller coaster of all-time.

"We told you, hon. I can't stay forever." In her name-brand sneakers and bike-shorts, Teagan hunkered down to speak with him eye to eye.

She'd received a call on her cell and Tate had overheard the result. Now Teagan held her brother's small arms while Dex stood by, suddenly over his cream-cheese pretzel.

"We can talk about it later," Teagan said.

"Later," Tate told her, "you'll be gone."

In Sydney, Cole spent time with Tate when he could, but Tate's other siblings weren't available to him on a regular basis. These past days, however, Tate had seen a lot of Teagan. At twenty-six, she could have been his mom, *and* she was hands-on. Eloise Hunter, on the other hand, left Tate's day-to-day needs to others. No matter how resilient the little boy was, wanting to keep Teagan close if he could was only natural, even with Shelby on standby, eager to tag team.

"Sweetheart, I have clients waiting for me home in Seattle," Teagan said, trying not to look guilt ridden, which she clearly was.

"I don't want you to go."

"What say, when you're finished visiting Dex, you come stay with me for a while? A friend has a boy your age. She runs the day-care center at my gym."

The corners of Tate's mouth flickered with a smile. "Can I come now?"

"I have to be somewhere tomorrow night," Teagan explained. "An important person asked me ages ago. It'd be rude to back out now."

Tears filled Tate's eyes.

While Dex was a nanosecond from sweeping the kid up and concocting some way they could hang out together here in Disneyland for a week, Teagan buckled.

"I'll skip tomorrow night," she said, "and stay here another couple days—" she glanced over "—if Dex and Shelby don't mind."

Dex shrugged. "Stay as long as you want."

But beneath the stoic face, Teagan was uncomfortable about missing her date. Was the important person a boyfriend? She hadn't mentioned anyone special. Could be a friend. Or a business arrangement. Yesterday, she'd let slip her health and fitness company had seen some recent problems. Maybe she'd put out feelers for a partner...someone to share the workload, responsibilities and expense.

"No, Tea." Being brave, Tate blinked back unshed tears. "You go."

"Nah." Teagan dusted off her little brother's shoulders. "It's just a dumb old game anyway."

"A baseball game?" Tate asked, and she nodded. "The Mariders? They're from Seattle," he said.

"You like the Mariners, Tate?" Dex asked.

"Me and Cole—they're our team. He likes 'em coz of the compass. I like the moose. He rides a yellow mower. We watched a game before I left." Tate tilted his head at an angle. "Cole's going on a trip with a lady. She said next time maybe I can come."

Dex's heart dropped. Poor kid. Must seem as if every other person wanted to bail on him. Lord, he wished life was simpler. Nothing he could do there. He could, at least, divert the conversation.

"Who wants a cheeseburger?" Dex said, tossing his pretzel in a trash can.

"I have another idea," Teagan said.

Dex zipped his lip. He'd seen that look before—the one his sister got whenever she made a decision that no one on God's green earth could change.

"What if we try to get another ticket to that game?" Teagan asked Tate. "Until I make a call, I can't promise, though. They're special tickets." She reached for Dex's hand and squeezed. "Mind if I keep him a week?"

"Of course I don't mind."

He only wanted the little guy happy, safe and well fed. Although living with Teagan, Tate might need to suck it up and survive on soy burgers for a while.

Tate put his arms out for a hug. When Dex lifted him up, a soft voice whispered at his ear, "Love you, Dex."

"Love you, too, buddy."

In movies, kids and dogs never failed to touch hearts. In real life, the tugs were even stronger. Dex drew away before his throat thickened more.

"Just try not to overdose on tofu. Your sister's sweet and all, but she has some gross eating habits."

"Promise." Tate's smile was back. "Can I go on one more ride?"

"Let's get a shot of you all together first." Shelby's eyes were glistening as she looked on and whipped out her cell. "I'll get one of you two first."

She snapped the boys, then all the Hunter "kids," followed by one of Tate alone with his sister. Then Teagan took the phone.

"You two," she said, addressing Dex and Shelby. "Arms around each other, please."

Since their secret, all-too-brief encounter, Dex had been on his best behavior, which had taken more than a dash of will-power. While normal male urges suggested he do precisely what Teagan suggested now and hold Shelby close, he forced himself to wait until she capitulated and came to stand beside him, her smile uncertain and eyes round, as if she were afraid someone might read their thoughts and learn about their clan-destine kiss.

But Teagan knew nothing about that brush of lips, or that he daydreamed about kissing Shelby again, only this time in earnest.

He and Shelby smiled, Teagan clicked and Dex exhaled. As Shelby might say, *done and finished*. Until...

He made the mistake of turning to Shelby at the same in-stant she looked at him. Their gazes fused and "say cheese" smiles faded as a visceral awareness swelled between them just as it had that night on the couch. Only the tug now was stronger, the pitch even higher. The bustle around them faded and all he could think about was the moment his mouth had grazed hers and, for a beat in time, she had kissed him back.

Then a noise broke through the fog and, coming back, Dex

looked around. Tate was making whooping sounds. He flipped a killer cartwheel and leaped up and down on the spot. To top it off, he spun around to shake his tail feathers.

What a performance! Everyone, including passersby, stopped to applaud and laugh. Holding her stomach, Shelby collapsed against Dex. In stitches, he lashed a bracing arm around her waist while Teagan's face and sides split, too.

Dex got it together enough to ask, "What's that all about? You auditioning for Mickey?"

"I knew you two liked each other," Tate cried out. "I *knew* it! You were gonna kiss Shelby and she was gonna kiss you back." Tate slapped both palms against his mouth then threw a giant air-kiss—and matching smacking sound—out for them both to catch.

While Shelby sobered, shaking her head as if she hadn't a clue what Tate was on about, Dex took a moment.

Tate was bright but he was five years old, for Pete's sake. If he could see how deeply Shelby affected him, things were bad. Or were they good? Because tomorrow, Tate—everyone's priority and main reason they had held off—was leaving for Seattle.

He and Shelby would be alone again.

"While Tate's away," Shelby said, "I'll bunk down at my place."

It was the day after Disneyland. Dex had just walked in the door, back from having driven his sister and little brother to the airport to catch their flight to Seattle. Now, standing in the center of the suite, a packed bag at her feet, Shelby felt strong—and justified—after voicing her decision.

Dex blindly set his key card on a credenza. "Tate'll be back in no time. You've already moved your stuff here."

"One bag. I kept my place for just this kind of situation."

"The kind of situation that puts us together alone?"

Shelby's breath caught. But if he could be blunt, so could she.

"You hired me to look after a child. Now, with Tate away, I'm not sure what I'm doing here."

He sauntered over. "And the rest?"

She lifted her chin. "And I know what you're planning. You promised to forget what happened between us the other night."

"I did promise, didn't I."

His words…the confident, almost predatory gleam in his eye…

She clasped her hands at her waist. "But with Tate gone and us here by ourselves…" As he strolled closer, those big shoulders rolling, she backed up. "You're planning to kiss me again. And…well…" *Be blunt.* "I'm afraid I might kiss you back."

If that happened, and things got out of hand, then turned irretrievably sour, she'd have no one to blame but herself.

That night when their lips had brushed, time had wound down, hormones had sat up and, for that moment, the urge to surrender it all had been hypnotic. They'd barely kissed and yet never in her life had she felt that level of raw sexual need. She'd been gripped so fast, so tight, and her reaction afterward had been just as fierce.

Perhaps the intensity was psychological more than physical…some kind of projection to help her cope with that other situation back in Mountain Ridge. Except, from the start, she'd known she was attracted to Dex. It turned out that the attraction was way more than she'd bargained for.

Reaching down, she swept the bag off the floor. "I don't want to complicate things."

As he came to stand before her, those wonderful, frightening feelings sparked again. Suddenly her breasts felt heavy; her brain began to buzz. But this was *not* what she'd signed on for, no matter how sexy, charming and convincing Dex Hunter might be.

When his fresh male scent slipped into her lungs, she held her breath and skirted around him. At the front door, she made herself crystal clear.

"When Tate comes back, so will I."

Leaning back against the sofa, he crossed his arms and ankles. Relaxed. In control. Insufferable and irresistible.

"What if you don't come back?" he asked.

"We have a contract."

"As if I'd sue if you break it."

"I don't work that way."

"Always by the book, huh?"

"That's right." She was honest. Sometimes too honest.

"And if I promise not to take advantage of the situation?"

But that would mean that she'd need to promise, too, and with this drugging heat sluicing over her skin and ticking inside of her, she simply couldn't. His tousled hair, crooked grin, the width of his chest beneath that sexy lilac button-down... Feeling the way she did now, merely looking at Dex was almost enough to undo her.

He'd asked would she stay if he promised to be good.

"Like I said..." She opened the door. "Too complicated."

He pushed off the sofa and ambled toward her.

"I have to admire your ethics. Perhaps I should take a page from your *Abstinence Is Best* policy."

That raised her hackles. Did she look like a virgin? Not that there was anything wrong with being chaste. "I have had sex before."

He rubbed the back of his neck as if he were suddenly overly warm. "I wish you wouldn't use that kind of language in front of me."

"Fine." Bag in hand, she stepped into the hallway. "While you drive me home, I won't talk dirty."

She was teasing. And she shouldn't. Because Dex didn't smile. In fact, his pupils had grown so that the tawny irises were almost consumed by the black. Actually *he* looked consumed. If he gathered her close now—if he stole a scorching kiss—would she find the strength to push him away? Principled or not, when his lips met hers, values got a little hazy.

When he crossed to the living room extension and called the

valet service, she released her breath. They drove to her address in relative silence. He saw her to the building's security door.

"You have a key card to my suite if you need it," he said, shoving his hands in his pockets. "You'll find wages in your account."

"I haven't earned them."

"Contract states wages will be deposited weekly for the next six months, no matter what. And don't forget, you're on call." When Tate got back.

"And don't you forget to eat your veggies," she chided. "Remember what I told Tate. They're good for you."

His grin grew as he shook his head and walked away. But he made sure she was through the security door and inside before he swung in behind the steering wheel and drove off.

Everything in the apartment was as she'd left it. Same cheap cotton sofa and vinyl recliner. Same Formica kitchen countertops and wooden table with someone's initials, *BL,* carved into one corner. In the bedroom, she winced at the dragging curtains. Hanging out in a Beverly Hills suite could spoil a girl fast.

She set the bag on the faded quilt, but paused before setting down her tote. Finally she opened the inside zipper and drew out the photo she'd almost lost the other day. Tracing a finger over those innocent smiles, she let a slipstream of memories take her back to a time when life had seemed so simple. When her mother was alive. When she believed in dreams and princes who rode white chargers.

The two girls in the photo weren't friends anymore. Never would be again. But that didn't erase their history. This photo had lived on her dresser for over a decade. And its twin?

Surely her onetime friend would have dumped it. She'd at least need to keep it out of sight. Reese wouldn't want Kurt to see, or for either of them to be reminded.

Was Reese ashamed of what she'd done? If roles had been reversed, Shelby wouldn't have been able to live with herself. She wouldn't have done it at all.

When her nose began to prickle, Shelby set the photo on the dresser and siphoned in a fortifying breath.

She ought to go shopping, fill the fridge. But, while she didn't feel much like staying in, she felt less inclined to go out. In the living room, she flicked on the television, flipped through some channels. A classic was showing. A romance.

The couple had fallen in love on a cruise. But their lives were complicated with other love interests. They vowed, if those complications got sorted out, they would meet again in a year's time. Riveted, Shelby curled up on the sofa and watched to the end. So sad, so beautiful. Of course, it made her cry. The hero had loved the heroine and nothing and no one could keep him from being with her.

As credits rolled, Shelby dabbed a tear with her sleeve and blinked around the room. For a minute, she'd forgotten. She was here in this drab apartment because she needed to preserve her and Dex's professional relationship in order to safeguard Tate's best interests. Except that Tate was with Teagan. Reese was with Kurt. And she was stuck here.

Principled and alone.

Seven

Home from work two days later, the minute Dex opened the suite door, he knew he had company.

As he entered the living room, he spotted that unmistakable tote and a big smile came over his face. Shelby was back and something delicious was sizzling on the grill. Thank God he hadn't dropped into a local haunt to chow down. Shelby's cooking topped near anything he'd tasted.

Whistling, filtering out from the kitchen, grew louder until she appeared, heading toward the polished dining table. In one hand, she carried cutlery, in the other, linen napkins. When she saw him, she stopped short before a grin kicked up one side of her beautiful mouth.

"I didn't know when to expect you," she said.

"I smell steak."

"Thick cut with mushroom gravy."

"Some people don't like mushrooms. I happen to love them. I have the perfect wine accompaniment." He moved toward the bar. "You do drink wine, don't you?"

"Sure. A little."

After washing his hands in the sink behind the bar, he un-corked a good red and brought the wine and two glasses to the table. Shelby was returning with plates covered with Texas-size steaks. Bowls of salad and creamy mashed potatoes already waited on the table. With his mouth watering—over the meal and also the cute tangerine-colored dress she wore—he pulled out her chair for her to sit.

"May I ask why you changed your mind?" He took his seat, poured the wine.

"Don't be offended, but I was bored."

"Isn't retail therapy a woman's preferred antidote to that?" He cut into the steak, took a mouthful and sighed at the blend of flavors and textures. Now he was glad he'd skipped lunch that day.

"I'm not big on retail therapy."

"Does that mean you've decided to hang around?"

Finished dressing their salads, she nodded and he raised his glass. *Excellent.*

"Let's toast to that."

Crystal *tinged* as their two glasses met. "To hanging around," she said.

"You make it sound like a sentence."

"Now you're fishing for compliments." After sipping, she set her glass down. "We need to agree on some ground rules."

"Sounds official."

"I'll prepare meals, take care of laundry needs. Just to be clear, this arrangement does not automatically include me jumping into bed with you."

"Nor, I imagine, you jumping into bed with me."

Her lips twitched. "Agreed." Looking relieved she'd got that out the way, she gestured toward his plate. "How's the steak?"

"Not so bad," he joked.

"For that you do the dishes."

"Isn't there a mechanical device for that?"

"I prefer to hand-wash and dry."

Sounded like a drag. But his second mouthful was releasing so many surges of dopamine in his brain, through his blood, to enjoy these pleasures—this meal, Shelby's company—he'd pay any price.

After dinner, Dex helped with the dishes, and actually enjoyed it. He would've suggested coffee and, perhaps, dessert, but Shelby seemed set on retiring—or was that escaping?

Not that he had any intention of coming on strong. Of stealing that long anticipated kiss. She'd come back to him. Hell, she'd missed him. But in Shelby's world that didn't come close to taking that next fateful step. He wouldn't push. Not enough to scare her away, in any case.

Later, getting into bed, he decided to get a good night's sleep without wondering what tomorrow with Shelby would bring. But he *did* think about tomorrow, like he thought about tangerine dresses and discussing his day with an unassuming but stimulating companion who listened with genuine interest rather than stars in her eyes.

He thought about that a lot.

The next morning, showered and dressed for work, he was fixing his tie when the aroma of coffee beans brewing teased his nostrils. He found Shelby in the kitchen, hand-beating batter for pancakes. Her hair sat whipped up high on her head but a single tendril hung down, long enough to almost bounce into the bowl as she beat. Her PJs were cut like a man's but made in a soft pastel pink with a cat stitched on a breast pocket. Not a scrap of silk or lace in sight but in this early light, with a faint pillow crease on her cheek, damn, did she look hot.

Glancing up, she blew that wave of hair off her face.

"Hungry?" she asked.

And for way more than pancakes, he thought.

He headed for the percolator and poured a cup of coffee. "I'll take a rain check. Early meeting," he explained.

Listening, she sucked batter off the side of her thumb in a deliberating way that made his groin give a jump. But he needed to concentrate on the upcoming meeting with Rance Loggins. Another script with potential had landed on his desk. Rance was back in town and Dex wanted his thoughts.

He downed his coffee. A drop fell on his white business shirt when he drew the cup from his lips. He rubbed the stain, then moved to the sink and wet his fingers before trying again.

"That needs a soak," Shelby said.

He stood back. "Can you see it?"

She nodded. "But laundry came back yesterday before you got in. There should be fresh…shirts…"

He'd wrung loose his tie, was flicking open his collar and the next button, when he noticed Shelby was watching his actions at the same time her words trailed off. Then her gaze snapped up to meet his, her cheeks grew pink and, grabbing the milk, she strode to the fridge.

While he slid his tie's noose over his head, she stayed at the fridge longer than necessary, apparently sussing out its contents. When she finally turned around, that smoky-slash-guilty look was still in her eyes. Her voice was a little husky, too.

"Will you be home for dinner?"

"I have a function."

She arched a brow. "Busy man."

"It's a dinner dance to raise money for a very worthwhile charity."

She blinked. "Oh, sorry. I'd thought it'd a premiere or awards ceremony or something less…humbling."

"The cost of the ticket was humbling enough." She returned his good-humored smile. "I can swing another one if you'd like to join me in supporting a good cause."

She gave a pained look. "I couldn't go to something like that."

Imagining her in an evening gown, a satiny flowing creation that did justice to her curves and her smile, he grinned. "You really could."

"You said you wouldn't expect me to mix in those circles."

"I'm not asking you to come as your boss, Shelby." He

staved off the urge to brush that curl back off her cheek, curve his palm around her warm nape. "I thought it'd be fun."

Passing him, she returned to her batter. "No."

"No, it wouldn't be fun?"

"No, I won't go." She switched on a stove element. "I'm sure you'll have plenty of dance partners to choose from."

"I'm not interested in dance partners."

"And why's that?"

"I don't dance."

She laughed.

"It's true," he said. "I have two left feet on a dance floor."

"I don't believe you." But then she stopped pouring batter into a heating pan to judge his open expression. She cocked her head. "When was the last time you tried?"

"Graduation night. There was a lot of pouting and tears. My date wasn't happy, either."

She smiled before her look turned earnest again. "The basic stuff is easy to learn."

"I manage fine without it."

"There are occasions when a man *needs* to dance."

"I'm living proof there aren't."

"What about a bridal waltz?"

That took him aback. He'd never thought about it. Why would he?

He was standing beside her, enjoying the aroma of pancakes but more enthralled with the scent of her hair. Wildflowers. Fresh. It was all he could do not to move closer and fill his lungs with even more of her.

As if reading his mind, she turned more toward the grill and shrugged.

"I thought you had a meeting."

He exhaled. "Yeah, I do."

"And you need to change that shirt." She wiggled her finger at his face and added, "You have toothpaste at the corner of your mouth."

He blindly rubbed a spot.

"Not there," she said. "*Here*."

She pointed but he must have missed again because she pulled her sleeve up over her hand and did the rubbing for him. She was concentrating, her face close. That strand of hair had fallen over her cheek again. Her skin was flawless and her eyes were so big and bright, sparkling in sunlight filtering in through the window.

She must have realized all his attention was pinned upon her. Her hand slowly lowered but her gaze remained on his mouth while the air between and around them began to steam. He shouldn't kiss her. Even if he should, this wasn't the time. So why was he moving closer? Why wasn't she stepping away?

His lips were a hair's breadth from hers when he moved to embrace her but his hand knocked the bowl of batter.

Shelby stiffened, jerked away and realized that batter in the pan was burning. She shunted the pan off the heat then went to work scooping batter back into its bowl while Dex growled at himself. Coffee stains, toothpaste smears, spilled batter. He wasn't normally clumsy but this morning he was a disaster waiting to happen.

"You don't want to be late," she said, dropping the bowl in the sink and washing batter from her hands.

She was right. If he stayed any longer, he'd break something…most importantly, her trust.

He was on his way out when she pulled him up with a question.

"How are those rats doing?" she asked.

He lived by the philosophy that problems only got worse if a person poked and fussed. He didn't do conflict unless a skirmish was unavoidable. Much better to shrug off an incident than plow anyone in the jaw. Her jerk ex-boss came close to being the exception to that rule. But what he wouldn't give to be able to knock flat the S.O.B.—the rat—who had set that mini-bonfire in his backyard.

He hadn't heard any more. Still, he was glad he'd organized those surveillance cameras. That scum might pull another stupid stunt before he realized Dex would never bow to those kinds of demands.

"The rats are under control," he assured her then, walking out, promptly putting the matter from his mind.

Around midday, Shelby received a call.

"There's an item waiting for collection at reception," Mr. Lipou, the hotel manager, said. "It's addressed to Ms. Shelby Scott."

For her. Was he sure?

In an ornate mirror hung on an adjacent wall, Shelby took in her attire then the tumble of hair she'd barely brushed. To work off tension since Dex—and his burgeoning animal magnetism—had left that morning, she'd baked nonstop. If there'd been a horse around, she'd have swung up into a saddle and thundered over a wide open plain until she was ready to fall off, exhausted.

Had she come back with the intention of starting something physical? Intimate? Blow-her-mind sexual?

Now that they were alone here together again, given the amount of sizzle whenever he got within kissing distance, the idea was becoming increasingly hard to resist.

In fact, the more cookies she'd baked, the more she'd thought that perhaps a scorching-hot fling might not be such a bad idea, after all. If a torrid affair with Dex Hunter didn't help her forget what had happened back in Mountain Ridge, nothing would. As long as she kept it all in perspective. Strictly short-term.

Hearts need not apply.

On the other end of the line, the manager was asking when she might collect the delivery.

"Could someone bring it up?" she asked. Patrons always looked so swanky; she felt out of place every time she walked through the lobby.

"I'm afraid that isn't possible," the manager said. "The delivery needs to be collected within the hour."

Before she could mention the fact that this was a five-star

hotel so surely they could drop a delivery off to a guest's suite, Mr. Lipou had disconnected.

A few minutes later, wondering what on earth could be so urgent, she stood at the massive reception counter. Feeling awkward in her denim shorts and a T-shirt, Shelby gave her name. After sliding open a drawer, the attendant handed over an envelope, which was embossed with the hotel's emblem. Moving to a corner of the bustling foyer, she pried open the seal.

Inside, printed on hotel letterhead, was a voucher for a purchase from the in-house boutique, as well as hair and makeup appointments to be redeemed that afternoon—all compliments of Dex Hunter. The postscript noted a limousine would collect her at 7:00 p.m.

Withering into an upholstered tub chair, Shelby held her damp brow. Dex had gone ahead and organized another ticket to that charity shindig. She'd been clear. She wasn't a socialite. She didn't like attention.

Well, she simply wouldn't go. The limousine could wait and wait and it wouldn't be her fault one bit.

She was striding back to the elevator when the name on an in-house store drew her eye. Let's Pretend, the same boutique mentioned in her letter. Curious, she glanced at the gowns displayed in the window—a black cocktail number, a fire-engine-red party frock. An evening gown that was so simple yet breathtaking and feminine and—

Shelby straightened.

Well, it was way too pretty for a woman like her.

"May I help you?"

A coiffed attendant stood at the entrance. Shelby mumbled, "No, thanks," and was ready to keep moving when the woman spotted the letter in her hand and asked, "May I?"

After perusing the letter, the attendant, dressed in an elegant cream linen dress, gestured her through the door.

"Mr. Lipou said to expect you, Ms. Scott. My name's Celeste." She studied the gown in the window then sized Shelby up. "That would look stunning on you."

Shelby wanted to laugh. Her? In that? Instead she surveyed the gown again.

"I've never worn anything like that before."

Taking Shelby by the arm, Celeste led her into the boutique. "While you try it on, I'll organize your hair and makeup." She squeezed her hand. "You're going to dazzle everyone tonight."

Eight

After he'd wrapped up for the day, Dex showered and changed into the tux and buffed shoes that he kept at his office. Humming the same tune he'd heard Shelby often whistle, he fixed his bow tie in the mirror, enjoying a ripple of excitement as he contemplated the coming evening. He'd teed up the extra ticket to the charity do, no problem.

The question was, would Shelby step outside of her safety zone and accept his invitation? She might be reserved but she would unwittingly charm anyone who crossed her path. She had what the industry termed *star quality*. Difficult to describe. Far harder to create. In his opinion a person was born with that kind of allure. He'd seen it in Shelby.

So had Rance.

Perhaps he would open a floodgate by introducing her to this crowd tonight. He wished her nothing but success, although privately he could confess to a level of selfishness where Shelby Scott was concerned. He wanted her for himself.

But theirs was a temporary arrangement. Like the rest of

the family, he was dedicated to helping their father with his current situation. But, hopefully, the maniac stalking Guthrie would soon be apprehended, Tate would fly home, and that would mean Shelby would move on, too.

Dex doubted her next assignment would be in child care. Hell, he wouldn't be surprised if she landed a marriage proposal. More than one. She could be stubborn, a bit self-righteous, but also incredibly committed with loads of common sense. Whoever landed her as a wife would be a lucky man, indeed.

Dex only prayed whoever she ended up with was the marrying kind. In this town too many relationships fell apart. Ego... the fast life...something better always beckoning around the corner... In Hollywood, there was never a dull moment. Always somewhere new to go. Someone more exciting to see.

When he arrived at the venue, the block was awash with beautiful people and flashing lights—the usual pizzazz. Standing well off to one side of the red carpet, he checked the time. The hotel manager had called earlier; Shelby had chosen a gown and accessories. Mike, the studio limo driver, had been instructed to wait in the forecourt. Mike hadn't called to say she'd declined the ride. Neither had Shelby left a message for him directly.

Absently checking his diamond-studded cuff links, Dex peered down the street. She ought to be here soon.

Half an hour later, arrivals were thinning. With formalities due to begin, he had to think about moving inside. He'd check with Mike first—make certain Shelby had been a no-show. But his cell phone buzzed before he could dial.

"Just checking in," Teagan said.

"All good with Tate?"

"He's having a ball. Dex, he's so adorable. I won't want to give him back."

"You never were good at sharing."

The only girl growing up in the Hunter household, Teagan had been showered with attention and privileges. As a teen, her wardrobe had outshone their mother's. Then again, Teagan had endured a long rough spell after a childhood accident that had resulted in a run of operations and hospital stays. It was no secret that the experience was a big part of the reason she had chosen the health and fitness industry as a vocation. Who would guess now that she'd been confined to a bed for too much of her first years?

"Uh, sorry?" she said down the line. "*I* wasn't good at sharing? Everyone fell over themselves to give gorgeous Dexy anything he wanted. Come to think of it, what's changed?" Her teasing tone sobered. "Dex, I had a call today from an insurance company. The man said you gave him a referral to contact me."

Dex craned up on his toes. Was that another limo snailing down the street? "One of those database foot-in-the-door jobs," he guessed.

"This man said you'd had a fire and that you'd been thankful it hadn't spread."

All Dex's senses seized as the world around him blurred and funneled into a shadowy background. He didn't breathe. Couldn't blink. Finally he swallowed.

"What did you tell him?"

"I hung up. I know you're Mr. Cool, but you'd have mentioned something as frightening as a fire, particularly with Tate set up to stay."

Dex was scrambling for a half-decent reply when Shelby's limousine pulled up and Mike alighted.

"I have to go."

"You're at a function? I hear the commotion. Who's your date? Shelby?"

"Why would you think that?"

"Tate isn't the only one who can see you two are hot for each other."

"On that note, I'll say good-night."

"Have fun." She laughed. "Then again, you always do."

Moving toward the gleaming stretch, his thoughts were far

from fun. His mind was still reeling at Teagan's news. The rat wasn't finished playing games, trying to get to him via his sister now. He needed to warn her.

And Tate?

He couldn't return to Australia. Wynn would have Tate stay with him in New York in a heartbeat. But if Teagan had been contacted, other family members, including Wynn, might be, too.

He didn't have any option.

It was up to him to keep his brother close and safe, and in the meantime pull out all stops to defuse this blackmail situation. Tomorrow he'd put a private detective on the job and organize security measures here and in Seattle for Teagan in case she needed it. In the meantime...he would make the most of this evening with Shelby.

She slid out of the car as if she were stepping out of an A-list movie poster. Her hair cascaded in shiny loose waves all the way down her back. Whatever smoky effect the makeup artist had used to accentuate her eyes left him bewitched. And that gown... His jaw must be hanging.

Her long legs angled out from beneath a midnight-purple satin dream of a dress as he helped her onto the pavement. He smiled into her glittering gaze. When she blew out a breath and smiled back, he tucked her arm beneath his and—placing those darker thoughts in another box for now—escorted her to the entrance.

"You know you'll leave every woman here for dead," he said. "Guests will want the name of this new Hollywood beauty."

"Just so you know," she told him as they wound between groups on their way to the ballroom, "I was angry you organized a ticket and dress and everything else."

"Still angry?"

With a small smile, she shook her head and those big glossy waves bounced around her shoulders. "Honestly, I feel like a princess."

"You carry yourself like one, too. Maybe you were abducted at birth from a little-known European royal family."

She rolled her eyes. "Your imagination is something else."

Still, it wasn't difficult to imagine her in haute couture full-time, turning heads as she breezed by. Shelby didn't have a clue how stunning she looked. Then again, she'd looked amazing in this morning's pussycat pajamas, too.

In the ballroom, Shelby's eyes rounded at the elaborate chandeliers, towering swag curtains and exquisitely dressed tables. Amid the noise of chatter, crystal champagne flutes pinging and background music courtesy of a twelve-piece band, they were ushered to a prime location near the stage. Five other couples seated at the table nodded and introductions were exchanged. After seating Shelby, as he pulled in his chair and turned to ask more about Shelby's day—Had the staff at the hotel treated her well? Had she found any other dresses she wanted put on the tab?—he felt a tap on his shoulder and edged around.

Dressed in a tux with a bright orange bow tie, Rance Loggins stood beaming—but not at Dex. At Shelby.

Rance addressed Dex first. "Should have known I'd find you here."

"If you'd made this morning's meeting," Dex returned, "I'd have mentioned it."

Rance hunkered down. "Shelby, you look stunning."

The glossy bows of her lips parted, most likely to downplay the compliment. But then she seemed to rethink.

Smiling graciously, she replied, "Thank you."

"The meeting slipped your mind?" Dex persisted. He didn't like the way Rance was looking at his date, like a bear pondering a pot of honey.

"Not as if you haven't rescheduled in the past," Rance replied. "There's plenty of time to work on this new project."

Dex sat back. Oh, now, there was *plenty* of time for scripts. He shuddered to think how much Rance would get done if Shelby took up his job offer.

Rance spoke to Shelby again. "After dinner and formalities, would you join me for a dance?"

Holding back a growl, Dex pushed to his feet. "The evening's getting underway. You need to return to your own company."

Rance rose to his full height, too, which brought his nose up to Dex's chin.

"I only ask because you'd rather catch the flu than foxtrot," Rance said. "And looking like she does tonight, Shelby deserves at least one spin around the floor."

"You don't think others will ask?" Dex pointed out.

The corners of Rance's mouth crimped up. "Friend, I'm certain of it."

Shelby cut in. "The lights are dimming. Someone's at the podium. I'll catch up with you later, Rance?"

Rance's focus shifted to Shelby and the tension steaming his glasses eased. "I look forward to it."

Dex sat down heavily and scooted in his chair.

"You okay?" Shelby asked.

His lips drew back from his teeth. It was meant to be a smile but, yeah, he was pissed. What kind of game was Rance playing? Did he want to continue to work with Hunter Productions? Because no matter how smitten Rance was, tonight Shelby was with *him*. Sure, Dex understood the appeal and Rance was a friend, but some people didn't know when to quit.

Like that freaking firebug who'd contacted Teagan pretending to be an insurance salesman. He couldn't wait for tomorrow to get started on straightening out that problem once and for all.

"Dex, darling, wonderful to see you. I don't believe I've met this young lady."

Dex explained the babysitting situation while the female visitor to their table listened, absorbed.

Despite her earlier reservations—and Dex's scowl when Rance had proposed a dance—Shelby was surprised and pleased with how the evening had turned out. Everyone at their table, as well as those who'd wandered over to catch up, were inquisitive about Dex Hunter's quiet but also polite and welcoming companion. Their most recent visitor, Minerva Vine, wore a galaxy of sapphires, which complemented a gown that belonged in the pages of *Vogue*.

"You've no modeling experience then?" Minerva asked Shelby. "And yet I sat glued to my seat as you entered the room. You move like you were born to own the catwalk."

Shelby managed a limp smile. "Can't be all those years I spent in a saddle."

"I was thinking more bathing suits than Stetsons." Minerva clicked opened her sequined pocketbook. "I head a modeling agency here in L.A. I'd love for you to stop by to discuss opportunities."

Dex smoothed the napkin on his lap. "I'm afraid Shelby's not interested in modeling."

And certainly not swimsuits.

"Thank you," Shelby said, "but my dad would keel over if he thought I was parading around half naked for all the world to see."

She couldn't imagine the rest of Mountain Ridge's reaction.

"Sweetie, in case you hadn't noticed," Minerva said, "that dress leaves little to the imagination, and what *is* left could compel every man in this room to crawl over cut glass to see more."

Shelby flushed down to the deep vee in her gown and probably to her knees.

Sure, this gown fit well. And, given the fabric and style, the boutique assistant had recommended that she forget the bra. Admittedly, at first she'd felt as if she were walking around in nothing more than a sexy slip of a petticoat. But she'd never meant to outright tease. Other than her arms, she was mostly covered. This gown wasn't *that* revealing.

Was it?

Minerva's manicured fingers tapped her bare shoulder. "Think about my offer. Take as long as you need."

When Shelby reached for the card Minerva had left beside her glass, Dex's hand enveloped hers. As he leaned close, his lighthearted words warmed her ear.

"It's a good thing I have you under contract."

That wouldn't have made a difference.

"I don't want to be a model," she said as his thumb skimmed across her jumping pulse before drawing away. "I can't think of anything more...not me."

"Still, Minerva's right. The camera would love you."

She drank in her glittering surroundings, their high-society company, and wondered at the ease with which she'd been accepted here tonight—a far cry from how she'd felt on that last horrible evening in Mountain Ridge. Then she'd been humiliated. A pariah. She loathed the thought of ever facing those people again. If it wasn't for her father, she'd never go back.

Although she'd had her reasons for choosing L.A., of course she had been anxious about such a big move. But had she truly found her new home? A place where others seemed to support her rather than speak in whispers behind her back? She could have lived in Mountain Ridge all her life; she'd had friends there. But juicy stories like hers lived on. So did the shame.

Between courses, various persons associated with the charity spoke about military families and how they remained close to their loved ones during times of illness or injury or disease after they'd returned from war. Shelby learned about marathons, galas, auctions, scholarships as well as individual fund-raising programs. Throughout each address to the audience, Dex's expression remained somber. She'd never seen him look more absorbed, or more handsome. Everything about Dex Hunter always seemed so polished, and the way he filled out that tuxedo...

Well, he ought to be a movie star himself.

When the last round of applause went up and the formalities were done, she asked him, "How did you get involved with this cause?"

"We all know someone who's sacrificed in one way or another. We're all affected—past, present. Future, too."

He sounded so sincere—so committed—she wanted to hug him. Far safer to rib.

"So, run any marathons for charity lately?"

"Oh, you should see me rip it out on a treadmill. Ten, even twenty, yards at a time."

He chuckled but she wasn't fooled. "You do it automatically."

He reached for his glass. "What's that?"

"Shrug off who you really are."

"I promise you, I don't run marathons."

Of course she hadn't meant that. "Beneath all the razzle-dazzle," she pointed out, "you're a sensitive guy."

He genuinely cared, and about things that counted. Social responsibility. Family, in all its guises.

Music was playing again and pinpricks of light had begun to revolve around the darkened room. Noticing couples filling up the dance floor, Shelby's thoughts veered toward Rance Loggins again. She adored dancing, but she was here with Dex—and, giddy as the notion made her feel, Dex was here with her.

As if reading her mind, his attention slid over to the dance floor, too. Beneath the cool facade, was he waiting for Rance to make his move? She didn't want to be the cause of trouble between friends—but she could fix that, for tonight, at least.

"Do you mind if we leave?" she asked. "I've had too much wine. My head's beginning to spin."

But before her excuse was fully out, someone else appeared at their table.

"May I steal this lovely lady away for a twirl around the floor, Dex?" The man spoke with an unmistakable Texan drawl. "I promise to return her." His lips twitched. "Or I promise I'll try."

Shelby replied before Dex could.

"We were about to leave."

The man, whom she recognized from more than one block-buster, gave an easy shrug. "I'll look forward to next time."

As the man sauntered away, Dex turned toward her. "I'm pooping your party."

"You're not at all."

"Go have a dance. Let me bring Owen back."

But when he pushed out of his chair, she held his forearm. The question slipped out before she'd thought it through.

"Would *you* like to dance with me, Dex?" She arched a play-ful brow. "I could lead."

Those tawny eyes gleamed. "Now, that does sound tempt-ing."

But he made no move to help her up from her chair. Deep down, she hadn't expected that he would. But, however flat-tering, neither did she want to be asked by anyone else. It was definitely time to go. She collected her pocketbook.

"Head still spinning?" he asked.

"I'm not used to all this."

"Do you think you *could* get used to it?"

When his lips hooked faintly up on one side, a thousand but-terflies were released in her tummy. She wanted to tell him no, she couldn't possibly get used to this kind of life. But not be-cause she couldn't wear gorgeous dresses, listen to wonderful music, drink exquisite wine every other night. As those lights spun around the room and Dex continued to smile into her eyes, suddenly she was overcome with a rather scary realiza-tion. The fact was she could get *very* used to all this, especially being with Dex this way, as if they were an item.

A true-life couple.

But soon Tate would return and her days would revert to having at least one foot set in reality.

Later, however, when they returned to the hotel suite in Bev-erly Hills, Dex explained that Teagan had called. It sounded as if Tate was having such a good time in Seattle, he might not *want* to come back to L.A.

Dropping his jacket over the back of the sofa, Dex added, "I told Teagan she couldn't keep him."

Shelby grinned. "What did she say to that?"

"Actually, I'll go up to collect him tomorrow."

For a moment, his brows knitted together. He looked so pre-occupied, even worried, she wanted to ask what was wrong. But then his slanted smile returned. He strolled over and his masculine scent began to seep in as it had when he'd sat next to her in the ballroom and during the drive home. Shelby had to steel herself against gravitating closer.

As his gaze skimmed her lips, her heartbeat skipped then began to race. Suddenly she was tingling all over, inside and out. He was letting her know again how he felt about her and this situation. Now was her opportunity to let *him* know she had started to feel the same way. Past tempted.

Beyond ready.

But her brain was all scrambled. The right words wouldn't come. Could this be as simple as coiling her arms around his neck and showing rather than telling? Because she longed to do just that. Press herself up against him…kiss those lips… make love all night.

And possibly get hurt?

Was she capable of having a purely sexual affair, an intimate relationship that kept the physical to the fore and shouted down emotions? How would she feel in the morning?

Confused, breaking away, she crossed to the balcony doors. She needed fresh air. He was right behind her.

"If it's the wine…" he said as she leaned against the rail and filled her lungs.

She couldn't meet his gaze. "It's not the wine," she murmured.

"Would you like me to leave you alone?"

Still staring at the lights below, she shook her head. After a trip-wire-tight silence, he spoke.

"You know how I feel about you, don't you, Shell?"

His low, deep voice… The way he'd said her name…

Shivering with longing, she held her nervy stomach.

She wanted this, but memories of that incident in Mountain Ridge kept slamming her in the face. Telling her to stop and be smarter than this.

"I'll be honest," he said, and as he angled closer, she sensed his grin. "This is serious. In fact, if serious had a big brother, this would be it. If I don't kiss you soon, it'll happen. I'll go stark, raving, loony-tunes mad."

That made her smile. Then his fingers trailed the back of her hand and blood rushed to the spot. At the same time, the tips of her breasts came alive and her legs turned to rubber bands. The ache low at her core was so sweet—so pure—she almost moaned.

"When I came to L.A.," she told him, "I promised myself I wouldn't get involved with anyone."

"Because of Reese and Kurt."

Her gaze shot up and fused with his. But she'd spilled enough the night they'd worked with Rance on that script. Of course, given his job, Dex would have put some pieces of her story together. Only the way she'd told it…

Her ending hadn't worked out that well at all.

"It's a long ugly tale," she said.

"If you ever need to talk about it…"

His hot palm was sailing up her arm. When he stepped into the space separating them—when her chin tilted up and she found his lips touching, brushing hers—the floor swayed beneath her feet. Everything around her seemed to slide and tip on its side. Unsteady, she held on to his dinner-shirt front.

"Maybe…" Her throat convulsed and she tried again. "Maybe we both have things we could share."

His palms cupped her bare shoulders. He searched her eyes for what seemed like an eternity before he pulled her close and, at last, his mouth captured hers.

The tenderness combined with intense heat left her blood steaming, her thoughts reeling. When the tip of his tongue slipped over the seam, her lips automatically parted. Still he kept the caress light, meaningful but also teasing. While time hung suspended around them, she soaked up the feelings of his fingers gripping her flesh, of her breasts brushing his shirt.

When he slowly broke away, she was buzzing, limp with longing.

"I've wanted to do that for a very long time," he told her.

Breathless, she cupped his scratchy jaw. "Well, don't stop now."

Her arms wound around his neck as his mouth covered hers again. A rumbling of satisfaction vibrated through his chest before the big palm on her back slid lower. His tongue swept over her lips, pushed past her teeth at the same time strong fingers filed up through the back of her hair, then lightly tugged. Her mouth opened wider, his head angled more, and a series of effervescent streams sailed like an angel's song through her veins.

This wasn't a kiss. It was a revelation. This man knew things others didn't. How to mesmerize. How to drug.

This time when his lips left hers, his mouth slid over her chin, then down her throat, where it settled on a pulse beating to one side. Giddy, she got a grip of his shoulders and dragged him almost close enough.

"Kiss me again," she murmured then released a sigh. "Kiss me everywhere."

His teeth danced across the slope joining shoulder and neck while his hold on her hip tightened.

"Tell me again." He nuzzled the sensitive spot below her ear. "Tell me what you want."

She admitted, "I want you."

She slipped the straps off her shoulders and the gown fell in a silken puddle at her high-heeled feet. Naked but for a thong, she tipped toward him again, eyes shut, lips parted and available. But he held her back.

"I might hate myself for reminding you," he said, "but you do realize we're outside on the balcony."

She blinked around. It was late, dark and, other than muf-
fled traffic noise below, quiet. Still...

"I should care, shouldn't I? Someone might see." People
might talk.

But he was already close again, his hand riding over the
rise of her behind. When those fingers slid between the backs
of her thighs, she clung to his shirt. Then she lifted one knee
and rubbed it along the outside of his thigh. A heartbeat later,
he was stroking the damp crotch of her underwear and she was
bearing down, rotating against him.

She let her brow drop against his shoulder but he angled her
face toward his and kissed her again, this time in a penetrating, thorough way that left her floating. And all the while his
fingertips skimmed and rubbed the thin strip of silk drawn
between her thighs.

When his stroke curled beneath the silk and a thick warm
finger slipped inside her, she shivered with want, sighing in
his mouth and fumbling for his buttons. As he pressed deeper
inside, his tongue wound faster, too. Sensations and emotions
whirled higher. Hotter. Light-headed, she gave up on civility
and wrenched his shirt wide apart.

Buttons popped and finally flesh met burning flesh.

As he maneuvered out of his shirt, her mouth left his to
graze lower over the broad hard plain of his chest. He tasted
so good. Felt so hard and hot. As the tip of her tongue trailed
around one flat nipple, her own breasts seemed to swell even
more. She found his other hand and, guiding it, helped him
cup her breast.

When the pad of his thumb circled that tight tender nipple,
a tingling rush shot to her core and her head lolled to one side.
Lost in the waves, she closed her eyes and arched back. His
arm around her back, he steadied her weight before his head
lowered to taste her.

While his tongue looped and teased that tip, she unzipped
his fly and tried to tug his trousers down. He nipped her nip-

ple and she bucked before he rotated them both and pressed her hard against the wall.

The brick was cool on her back while his mouth scorched her lips. As an almost unbearable need surged through her system, he broke the kiss to nuzzle her chin then dot urgent kisses along her jaw, across her cheek.

In her ear, he rasped, "Is this okay?"

She gave him her answer by finding his hand, slapping it under her behind and rocking her hips forward. Then she drove her hand between their bellies and locked fingers and thumb around his engorged length. As she worked his erection, the hand cupping her rear lifted her bit by bit until her toes nearly left the ground. A few seconds later, a big palm smacked the wall beside her cheek and his head jerked away.

His smile was half grimace. "What you're doing..." His hand fisted as his eyes clamped shut. "It's very distracting."

"In a good way, I hope."

"Almost too good."

He hoisted her up and her legs twined around his hips. When he eased her weight down slightly, she shifted the crotch of her thong and the tip of his length pushed an inch inside. The sensation snatched her breath away...left her senses swimming. In that moment, she felt unbelievably free, as if any world outside of this had evaporated into stardust. His chest hair tickling the points of her breasts...his hot scent infusing and exciting her...

And then he began to move, pumping a controlled rhythm that wound her ever higher. Each time he thrust, her hips pulled away before coming back to slap against him. With her arms latched around his neck, she kissed him deeply, unrelentingly, her tongue darting around his while his erection filled her again and again.

The friction was set to combust when, suddenly, his every muscle seemed to seize and his mouth dragged away from hers. One arm supporting her weight, the other hand braced against the wall, he strained to pull in each breath. She searched his face, his dark immersed gaze.

"I'm not wearing protection," he ground out.

That brought her back. He lowered her weight until she stood on her own two feet, albeit unsteadily. While she leaned against the brick wall for support, Dex moved—she thought to sweep something off the floor. But then she felt his breath warm at the apex of her legs. Two palms feathered up the inside of her thighs before he tugged the thong down enough for him to freely stroke and tease her folds.

Moist slow kisses dropped on her belly as two fingers slid into her opening. While she melted, he massaged a place just inside of her, and when she was quivering, biting her lip to hold back the whimper, his thumb lightly circled *that* place... a woman's most sensitive spot.

Sparks shot in every direction before falling around her to smolder and burn. She was unraveling, coming quickly apart. His lips grazed that spot, back and forth, round and round. She held her breath until it came out in a rush at the same time that burn turned white-hot.

She imagined his smile before the stiff tip of his tongue twirled around the base of that nub then flicked the sensitive tip and didn't stop. Sensations—sizzling and intense—whipped her around as her fingers knotted in his hair and urged him closer still. When his mouth covered her completely and he gently sucked, she began to tremble...then to shake.

Perspiration broke out, cool on her brow, between her breasts. She released his hair to clutch the wall at her back as her heartbeat grew louder and the heat continued to build. When his head angled and he pressed in more, the combination flipped a delicate switch deep inside of her.

Her ceiling blew sky-high.

Relishing every second, Dex held on as Shelby shuddered against him. He only hoped no one had a telephoto lens capturing all the action. Usually he kept this kind of activity indoors. He'd gotten carried away. Clearly Shelby had, too.

He should have known she'd be this hot.

Gradually the waves of her climax ebbed. Her grip on his head eased and loving fingers stroked through his hair. Then, spent, she began to slide. He whipped her underwear down her legs and flicked it away before sweeping her up into his arms and carrying her to his bed.

Moments later, he laid her down then drew the quilt from underneath her until she rested on the sheet. After finding protection in the bedside drawer, he sheathed himself and ditched his shoes and unzipped trousers while studying her, courtesy of the moonlight slanting in through the patio windows and glass doors. Her body seemed to glisten, her hair was a tangle and her dreamy smile told him she was completely satisfied.

In a languid movement, she arched toward him, asking him to join her. He slipped off her heels, then positioned himself between her legs. Kneeling, he eased up closer so that her thighs were drawn wider apart. His palms traced over her patch of curls before drifting higher to skim her belly. Ticklish, she smiled and bucked a little.

His palms swam higher, molding over her breasts. As her arms coiled up around her head, he rolled and plucked her nipples until her eyes drifted closed and her head rocked to one side on the pillow.

In plain language he hadn't expected from her lips, she asked him to take her. Happy to oblige, he lowered his head, twirled his tongue around each nipple in turn then, settling down, steered the tip of his erection inside of her again.

Just like the first time, primal pleasure ignited and slashed through his system. She fit him so well, and when he began to move, her walls seemed to grip and draw him in deeper. Moving above her, propped up on an elbow, he brushed a wave of hair off her cheek and searched her face, her satisfied smile.

He dropped a soft kiss on her brow, her temple, her cheek and ear, while the concentrated burn in his groin grew at the same time it compressed. When her legs coiled around the backs of his thighs and her nails drew goose-bumpy lines up his sides, his toes curled into the mattress. It all felt so good. *Too* good.

"Something wrong?" she asked.

He dropped a lingering kiss on her lips before his mouth trailed down one side of her perfumed neck. As he began moving again, he murmured in a slightly strained voice, "Everything's perfect."

Her legs pressed against the backs of his thighs, urging him to go deeper, while her warm palms drew leisurely arcs over his pecs, grazing his nipples with each brush…such simple actions that had his every tendon clenching and the room temperature soaring into the red. Then she craned up enough for her tongue to reach and circle the hollow at the base of his throat. Round and round, then a little flicker.

His length began to pound.

As their hips continued to meet, those nails grazed down his sides again. The push below had him biting down, fighting to hold back the tide. When her touch skimmed the inside of his hip bones, he grabbed both her hands and pinned them on either side of her head.

"You didn't like that?" she teased.

"You know exactly how much I like it."

"So much, you have to manacle me."

"If I didn't, this would be over way too soon."

Her legs roped higher behind him at the same time her hips ground up. Then her pelvis rotated and inner walls squeezed while her sultry gaze gauged his reaction and he spasmed more than once. He half laughed, half swore, before he admitted defeat and gave himself over to the inevitable.

He caught her left leg under the knee and brought her thigh back toward her stomach. Then he shifted higher, pumped deeper. Sweat beaded low on his back, across his brow, as he concentrated only on sensation…on the push building in his groin as he thrust again and again.

On another plane, he knew she was holding his face, that

her fingers were tracing the back of his ears. Her gentleness only made him that much harder.

He grabbed her other leg and positioned it the same way, knee bent, limb pressed toward her torso. As the mattress continued to rock, her fingers fell away. His heartbeat pounding, he opened his eyes and watched her climb again, lips parted as her breasts shook with each plunge.

The heat was blistering. His brain didn't work other than the basic signal to keep her pinned and happy beneath him. He wanted her to orgasm this way. He needed her to cry out his name.

When she did, his own climax tore through his veins like a firestorm. Focused on sensation—on the rush of pleasure—he was aware of her squeezing and contracting around him as they followed each other, shooting over the edge.

Nine

"I was in love once," she told him. "We were supposed to get married. It didn't work out. Hear it happens a lot."

They lay together draped in soft shadows, basking in the afterglow of their lovemaking. Her cheek rested on his chest; his arm hung, comfortable around her. Beneath the coverlet, his body felt so hard and warm. Curled up against him like this—revealing hurts and scars while his chest rose and fell on the steady stream of his breathing—Shelby felt safe in a way she hadn't for a long time.

When he'd stroked her arm a minute ago and asked her why she'd left Mountain Ridge, for once she hadn't considered dodging. He already had a fair idea. A failed love affair. A broken heart.

Pressing a lingering kiss to her crown, he urged her closer. "Whoever he is, the guy was nuts to let you go."

Did Dex want to know the details? The truth behind the most embarrassing episode of her life? When she'd told Lila at the café, her waitress friend had been appalled. Then she'd hugged her and said she had nothing to be ashamed of. Nothing at all.

Dex, on the other hand, might see her actions that night as slightly hysterical. Particularly if she admitted her darkest secret…what had happened *after* she'd shocked the town with her announcement. She could barely believe it of herself. What would her father say? Her mother, if she were alive?

But everyone had secrets, Shelby decided as she drew aimless patterns through the hair on his chest. There was definitely something secret she'd like to know about Dex. Something he'd avoided talking about from that first day she'd agreed to work for him. Shifting, she rested her chin on the bed of her fist.

"Tell me about those rats in your basement."

His body seemed to lock down and his, arm stiffened around her. Beneath her hand, his heart began to thump. After a few seconds, he pushed himself up to sit back against the pillows. He ran a hand through his tousled hair.

"If it's too private…" she began.

He studied her hard. "Sure you want to hear?"

She sat up, too. "Yes. Yes, I do."

"Years ago," he began, "I got caught up with a friend's problem. He was let go from his job over tales spun by an ambitious colleague. It ate at him. It was all he thought about, talked about. And he couldn't seem to get back on his feet. He was great with figures. Helped me out when I needed it. But for one reason or another, he missed out on every job he went for."

"You didn't offer him a job with you?"

"I thought about it. Frankly, I didn't like his frame of mind. Then he started to gamble. I should have known something bad would go down."

She sat straighter while he flicked on a bedside lamp.

"I gave him my time and a whole pile of cash," he went on. "In the end, I told him he needed to speak to someone. A professional. That night he threatened to set fire to his ex-employer's factory."

"Arson?"

"He'd called me from the site. Told me again those bastards needed payback. I said to stay put. That I'd come straight over and get him. I begged him not to do anything stupid. When I got there, the place was already alight."

"Was anyone hurt?"

"Thank God, no."

"How long does he have to serve?"

Dex looked down. A pulse began to jump in his jaw.

She brought the covers higher around her neck. "You kept his secret?"

"And now someone else knows I was there. I've got a couple of pay-up-or-pay-the-consequences threats. They wouldn't go to Joel. He can barely take care of himself let alone save a dime."

"And you haven't gone to the police about the threats?"

"There'd be questions." He exercised his neck as if to work out a crick. "I haven't seen Joel in a good while. It's not my job to toss him on the coals to roast now."

"What kind of threat made you move out of your home?"

"A foot-high replica of a coffin smoldering in my backyard."

Wincing, she held her roiling stomach. "That's sick."

"There was a note earlier. To buy their silence, I needed to leave a bag of unmarked bills in a certain Dumpster."

"You're not thinking of paying?"

"The date they specified came and went. I had hoped that they would move on. But whoever's behind it all contacted Teagan today, pretending to be an insurance agent. He said I had referred him and mentioned a fire that thankfully hadn't spread out of control."

Her stomach roiled more. "What are you going to do?"

"Warn her and get some protection. I'll contact the guy who's looking after my father's situation. One of Cole's long-time friends. Brandon might be able to recommend a private investigative firm."

"But Tate…you said you were going to collect him tomorrow. Bring him back. Do you think that's safe?"

"I'd rather Tate be here with me where I can keep an eye on him. I'll take time off from the studio until it's all settled."

"Who do you think it is?"

"Joel must have told someone…a family member, another friend. Plots for extortion go on more often than people might think. Some deadheads figure why work if they can sit back and rip someone else off."

Shelby agreed with that to the depths of her being.

"Have you ever thought," she said, "that if you turn your friend in, he might get some help?"

"As in help to survive on the inside, because that's what he'd need."

Shelby's face and neck grew hot. But wasn't there a difference between snitching and bringing the truth to light? Sometimes speaking out could help a friend…or ex-friend, as the case may be. Even if it hadn't worked for her.

But this wasn't some small town affair. "Dex, these kinds of people can get desperate. Look at your father's situation."

"This lowlife isn't out to hurt anyone. Just frighten them into handing over some change if he can. When I track him down, we'll have a chat. I'll make him see that it's in everyone's best interests to drop this and disappear from my life." His eyes gleamed at the thought. "When we meet face to face, he'll listen to reason."

Resting her cheek against his shoulder, for everyone's sake, Shelby hoped so.

The next morning, after a two and a half hour flight, Dex landed in Washington state. Arriving at Teagan's house, he asked the cab driver to wait. When his rapping on the front door received no response, a sick, creeping feeling filled his gut. Earlier he'd called Teagan to briefly explain what lay behind the bogus phone call from that so-called insurance agent. Then he'd said he was coming to get Tate.

Teagan had argued. After what she'd just heard, if Seattle wasn't safe, surely L.A. was worse. But Dex reassured her; he was taking time off from the studio, hiring a bodyguard and P.I. Tate would be under his personal, around-the-clock care.

Now, as he thumped the door again, Dex's blood pressure rose. Teagan was expecting him, so where the hell was she? Had the fire rat tracked down more than Teagan's phone number? Had something happened to his sister? To Tate?

Dex was about to stalk around the back to investigate when the door opened. Tate stood on the other side, a big bright grin on his face. Dex swooped the boy up into his arms. His palm cupping the boy's small warm head, he held his brother close.

"Where's your sister?" Dex said in a thick voice.

"I'm right here."

Dex opened his eyes. Teagan was waiting, her thick blond hair pulled back in its trademark ponytail, her expression concerned. Dex stepped into the foyer and closed the door before setting Tate on his sneakered feet. Teagan squeezed her little brother's shoulder.

"Go get your knapsack, sweetie."

"But Dex is here!" Tate gripped his brother's hand.

"You're going home with Dex," Teagan pointed out. "You can catch up on the plane ride back." Teagan had her 'not budging' look in place, so Tate scurried off. When he was out of earshot, Teagan gave Dex a hug before stepping back to study him. She winced.

"You're white as a ghost."

"Goes hand in hand with heart failure. What took you so long to answer?"

"I was finishing a phone call. Tate knows he shouldn't ever open the door by himself."

Now more than ever, a great rule to enforce.

"When I get back, I'll organize a bodyguard for you, too."

"No need."

"Hopefully not. But I'm not taking any more chances."

"I mean I've taken care of security. Or, rather, a friend of mine has. That's who I was on the phone to."

"What friend?"

"Someone who's concerned and insisted that he help."

"This isn't a subject to bandy around the coffee table. It's serious."

"Which is why I cannot believe you kept it to yourself this long."

"I mentioned it to Cole. I spoke to him again this morning to give him a heads-up before I called Brandon. He passed on a recommendation for a security mob for Seattle as well as in L.A."

"Like I said, Damian will take care of things up here."

She didn't get it. "This problem needs a heavyweight, not one of your gym jocks who depends on protein bars for added muscle."

Teagan laughed then apologized when Dex growled. "Sorry. But if you knew this particular friend, you'd understand. He's a capable guy."

The same guy she had needed to see last week? How well did she know this man? Call him paranoid, but suddenly Dex sensed a snake slithering under every rock.

He was about to ask more when Tate came barreling back, his dinosaur knapsack swinging at his side. Reaching them, he roped an arm around Teagan's leg and looked up with eyes that could melt an ice fjord.

"Wish you could come, Tea," Tate said.

"Not this time." Her ponytail swept over one shoulder as she bent to brush a kiss atop his head.

"Maybe you *should* come with us," Dex said.

She exhaled. "I have a business to run."

"And that friend watching your back," he added, still suspicious.

She released a warm smile. "Exactly. Check in when you get home. And say hi to Shelby." Teagan's brow furrowed. "She's still in the picture, isn't she?"

"Very much so."

And while he was sorry that she was involved in this mess, he was glad to have Shelby Scott on his side. She was sensible, committed…and what they had shared last night was also pretty darn amazing. This morning, after they'd made love again, he wished he could have stayed longer. She felt so right in his arms…the sensations she aroused where like nothing he'd ever experienced before. Perhaps it was due in part to the uncertainty, his unease over this situation, but he couldn't wait to get back to her…hold her, kiss her and make certain she was all right.

But with Tate moving back into the suite, their relationship would need to revert to hands off. Shelby had said as much herself this morning before he'd left. They'd reaffirmed their pact. As difficult as it would be to restrain those emotions, Tate's well-being in all things took priority.

Home from Seattle, Dex let Tate into the hotel suite. A heartbeat later, he spied the elaborate display laid out near the living room just as Shelby appeared, a welcoming smile spread over her face. She said hi and added, "I've baked some cupcakes especially for you, Tate."

"Can I have one now?" Tate said earnestly, hanging back a bit. "My stomach's grumbling."

"You can have two," Dex qualified, "if that's okay with Shelby."

"I'll help you put your stuff away first," she said.

Tate held his knapsack tightly in front of him. "I can do it."

Dex and Shelby exchanged a look before, with garnered vigor, she moved toward the living room. "I picked up something while I was out today." She nodded toward the mini prehistoric world Dex had spotted earlier…a spooky volcano, a swamp as well as an assortment of ferocious plastic dinosaurs.

Tate dropped his bag, ran over and scooped up a foot-high replica of a creepy creature Dex recognized from the original *King Kong*.

"*T. rex!*" Tate cried.

"And a pterodactyl and a couple of—"

"Stebasaurus!"

Shelby laughed. "Stegosaurus, yes. I think they're my favorite."

Shelby knelt down beside Tate but, concentrating on the dinosaur—or feeling a little crowded—he quarter-turned away. Shelby hesitated before tacking up her great-to-see-you smile.

Dex moved forward. "Go clean up, chum, and we'll wash those cakes down with a big glass of milk." When Tate lowered the *T. rex,* Dex said, "Take him with you, if you like. He's yours."

Tate blinked. "For keeps?"

"Uh-huh."

"Santa got me one," Tate explained. "He moves and growls. He sleeps on my bed." Tate held *T. rex* high. "But this one's even better. His skin feels like *slime.*"

As Tate strode off to his room, Shelby apologized.

"Hope you don't mind a Jurassic Park in your living room."

"If Tate's happy, I'm happy."

She pushed to her feet and joined him. "He looks a little lost."

"He was so excited on the plane. Didn't stop yabbering."

"It's me he feels uncomfortable with."

Dex knew the rules. No touching, definitely no kissing, while Tate was here. But his brother was out of the room and Shelby needed reassurance...the kind that involved holding her in his two arms and speaking warm words.

He drew her near. She stiffened but then relented and leaned against him.

"It's silly," she said against his shoulder. "I've worked with tons of kids. I was shy myself growing up. Still am, really. And Tate's been shuffled around so much lately."

He lifted her chin and smiled into those gorgeous green eyes. "This isn't your everyday, garden variety babysitting gig." He admitted, "We're all a bit on edge."

Her gaze searched his. "I'm just wondering...with you taking time off from the office, maybe it's best if I bow out. You know, leave you two alone."

"If I thought that was best for Tate, I'd tell you." His fingertips filed around the curve of her cheek. "But you and me and Tate... From the minute we started talking that day at the café, I knew we'd make a great trio." He dropped a kiss on her nose. "Just give him time."

When he heard the bathroom faucet shut off, Dex reluctantly released Shelby's waist and she left for the kitchen. Dinosaur tucked under one arm, Tate reappeared. Tacking up his smile, Dex rubbed his belly.

"I'm ready for those cupcakes."

"And tomorrow it's Disneyland."

"Not tomorrow, I'm afraid."

"Next day?"

"We'll see."

"Or the beach. I can body surf and tread water for almost two minutes."

"First things first," Dex said as Shelby brought out a tray. He gave a dramatic interpretation of a big cat's prowl following her to the table. "I call dibs on the jumbo one with the chocolate frosting."

His eyes round, Tate was already pulling out a chair at the table. But when he sat down, his expression slipped. "Tea says I shouldn't have too much cake or candy."

Tate slid an apprehensive look toward Shelby, who seemed to hold her breath before pouring three glasses and offering the perfect response.

"After you finish your milk," she said, "I think we should phone your sister. She might be missing you."

Tate's face glowed. "And phone Mommy and Daddy too?"

Dex dropped the chocolate-frosted cupcake on a plate and slid it in front of their pint-size guest. "You got it."

A couple of calls was easy. Disneyland at this point, or any other outing, didn't sit so well, even in the company of the bodyguard he was putting on duty tomorrow. Naturally Tate wanted to run around and spend time in the sunshine. But best to keep Tate indoors and über-close until he could get to the bottom of this situation.

When Tate gave a small smile and offered his *T. rex* to Shelby to hold while he started on the cupcake, Dex exhaled on a smile and sat back in his chair. Like he'd told Shelby—and she well knew—this wasn't "everyday." But as Tate and Shelby began to chat about massive meteors and the tragic demise of dinosaurs, Dex reassured himself.

Baby steps. They'd get through this, and get through it together.

Shelby was glad that Dex had hired a private investigator he had faith in. She was less happy about the stony-faced bodyguard who followed on their heels if ever they ventured outside of the suite. Which was rarely.

Shelby understood and supported Dex's mission to keep Tate safe at all costs. What she questioned was whether the five-year-old should be in his care at all during this time. Perhaps this situation wasn't as dangerous as the bullets and bashings Dex's father had endured in Sydney. Still, more than once she'd suggested that Guthrie Hunter needed to know about the trouble here so that he could make an informed decision about where he wanted his youngest son placed. But Dex was determined not to add to his father's worry. He was certain this less critical situation would be ironed out soon.

As the days wound on with no leads, Shelby wasn't so sure.

Still, in Tate's company she was always upbeat, and, thankfully, Tate had warmed to her…sharing stories about his friends back home, asking her to read to him at night. It nearly broke her heart when she'd tuck him in and he'd squeeze shut his eyes before mentioning his family in his prayers, particularly Teagan.

A week after Tate had come back to stay, Shelby saw an advertisement for a gallery exhibition and she had an idea. After breakfast, when Tate had taken himself off to play with his indoor putting set, Shelby asked Dex if he'd like to go.

Dex looked up from a studio spreadsheet he was studying on his laptop.

"Tate would be bored witless."

"I meant you and me. I thought Teagan might like to pay a quick visit. Tate would love that."

Dex frowned. "We ought to keep our heads low for a while longer. Teagan can come visit another—"

"Teagan's coming to visit?"

Tate had wandered out from his room. Now, at the prospect of seeing his sister, he started hooting and shooting around the living room like a firecracker.

Dex tried to calm him down. "I didn't say Teagan was coming to visit."

"You did. I heard. You said Teagan could come."

Shelby brought over Dex's cell phone. "No harm in asking."

"She'd need to take time off work."

"I'm sure she wouldn't mind playing hooky one day."

Dex sent over a slanted grin. "Tell you what. You ask her."

Tate had stilled, his big eyes glued on her, waiting for her response. He looked so hopeful and little and dependent on her. Shelby shucked back her shoulders.

"Get her on the line."

But when the call went through and a man answered the phone, Shelby was taken aback.

"Sorry," she said. "I must have the wrong number."

"You're after Teagan," the man said. "She's right here."

The man's voice was smooth, deep and confident. When Teagan got on the line, Shelby couldn't help but notice that her voice was a little husky.

"I hope I'm not interrupting anything," Shelby said.

Teagan was quick to reassure her. "Not at all. Just some… business I was wrapping up." She hurried on. "What's up?"

Shelby explained the situation.

"I know it's a weekday," Shelby went on, "but if you could possibly swing it, Tate would love to see you."

Shelby studied Tate's darling expectant face as he waited for a response. A reply didn't take long.

"I'll be down by noon tomorrow."

Shelby immediately boomed out the news. "She's coming!"

Tate took a breath then went straight back into firecracker mode.

The next day, as promised, Teagan arrived and Shelby and Dex went to a contemporary showing at a Culver City art gallery. Dex had insisted on buying her an outfit for the occasion; given that she had instigated this, she didn't feel she could refuse. He'd ended up putting half a dozen knock-out dresses for her on his card. For tonight she'd chosen a white brushed-silk dress, knee-length and modest, with a tasteful diamond cut-out at the décolletage. The matching pocketbook had been dipped in crystals.

Enjoying each other's company, and the art on show, she and Dex were talking to a couple who owned a stud-farm in San Miguel. They were interested in hearing about Shelby's life growing up on a ranch and were discussing organizing a day for her, Tate and Dex to visit when Shelby's cell phone signaled an incoming. She peeped at the caller ID.

And her chest tightened.

Since leaving Mountain Ridge, she and her dad had spoken regularly. Why was her father calling this time of night? His usual bedtime was not long after sundown. Muttering an excuse, she ducked off to hide in a quiet corner and take the call.

"Anything wrong?" she asked.

"Not a thing," her dad replied. "Just hadn't heard from you this week. I wanted to make sure you're okay. Los Angeles is a big city."

She apologized. "I've been busy."

Her father knew she was working as a nanny, taking care of a gorgeous little boy called Tate.

"Sounds as if it's all working out for you then," he said.

"How about you? Daddy, you sound so tired."

His voice was low and kind of creaky. She could imagine him in his easy chair, a dish of his favorite nut candy on his lap. Her mother used to sit with him in the evenings, watching her favorite sitcoms and romance movies. Shelby often thought her father turned on the television at night now purely for comfort's sake, dreaming that his dear wife was with him still.

"I'm not tired so much as getting long in the tooth," he said.

Sixty-one wasn't that old.

She had an unsettling thought. "You're not having those pains again?"

After some trouble, he'd had a stent put in five years ago.

"It's not the ticker," he assured her. "I'm fighting fit."

Still, tomorrow she'd phone Mr. Kokavec, a neighbor, and ask if he could look in on her father. Zeb Scott rarely went into town. He wasn't a man who asked for help, even when he really needed it. She wished she could be there now to make certain this uneasy feeling was nothing more than her imagination.

Then he started to cough. She was reminded of her own recent experience when she'd been laid up in hospital with a bad chest infection, and her heart dropped.

"That sounds bad."

He coughed a couple more times. "Damn bug just flew down my throat," he wheezed.

"You're on the porch?"

Dex appeared at her side. His smile fell when he saw her expression.

"I'm looking at that old tractor," her father was saying. "An eyesore. I should get rid of it but I like keeping her around."

Shelby sighed. Her father was looking to broken-down equipment for company now? She knew children left their homes. It was part of a normal life cycle. But it was that much harder when your parent was alone and living miles away from another living soul.

"Are you still playing cards Tuesdays at Dan Walton's?" she asked.

He chuckled. "Don't worry about babying me. I just wanted to hear your voice before I took myself off to bed."

She glanced around. The crowd was ebbing out the doors. The gallery was closing.

"Can I call you tomorrow?" she asked.

"We've caught up. Call next week. If I see Mrs. Fallon, I'll tell her you said hi."

Remembering Mrs. Fallon's kindness hiring her at the kindergarten, always taking an interest in her life without seeming to pry, Shelby smiled. "Do that. Talk soon."

Dex threaded her arm through his. Out in the open, he stopped to bring her wrist to his lips.

"You look like you're about to cry," he said.

"My dad sounded so odd on the phone. I wonder if he's well."

He considered her for a long moment. "Teagan's staying the weekend. You should fly down for a visit."

The thought of facing that town sent her pulse rate spiking. But she would feel better if she could see for herself that her dad—her only living immediate family—was okay. She didn't have to leave the ranch. And, hell, if people knew she was in town and wanted to talk, they could go right ahead and gossip.

"I can go tomorrow," she said. "Be back Monday."

"Take as long as you need. Tate and I will be here when you get back."

"You could take him to Disneyland while I'm gone." Tate asked to go every day.

Dex shook his head. "Too many people."

She read his thoughts. *Too many risks.*

And that's when the idea hit.

"You should come. Tate, too. I could show him how to ride a horse." Thinking of the individual Dex termed "the rat," she added, "No one will even know we've gone."

He studied her expression as if he thought she might be joking. "You want us to go to Mountain Ridge?"

"Tate could get out in the open, run around, meet my dad.

He'd have a ball." She arched a brow. "I bet you'd enjoy yourself, too."

"I always enjoy myself whenever you're around."

Then he drew her into the circle of his arms and, his mouth dropping over hers, gave a sizzling example of his enjoyment. The kiss was slow and hot and brought to the surface all those urges they had both tamped down these past days. When his hold tightened a fraction and the caress deepened more, she grew limp even while her heart began to thud against her ribs. She'd missed his touch so much. For so many reasons, she was glad that she'd suggested that Teagan take care of Tate tonight. And if Dex agreed to go to Mountain Ridge, she knew her dad would take Tate under his wing, show him the many wonders of the Scott ranch. He'd always wanted a son. A grandson, too.

And it might be selfish, but she and Dex might find some time to share by themselves…times like the one they were sharing now when she only wanted to have him all to herself.

When their lips gradually parted, Shelby felt her smile to her toes.

"Does that mean you'll go?"

His warm lips brushed hers again. "Let me get some stirrups for my boots and we'll book a flight."

"You mean spurs."

Clearing his throat, he steered her toward the car. "Yeah. Them, too."

Ten

They landed at the closest airport midmorning the next day and were driving through downtown Mountain Ridge by noon. Tate had chatted constantly but, worn out, he now slept in the back of the rental. In the passenger seat, Shelby held onto her seat belt and simply gazed out the window, watching people as they rolled down a wide small-town road. Dex hoped this would be a good time for her. A good time for them all.

"The first traders came here in 1871," she told him. "The newspaper and post office followed five years later. We were a site for public lease options during the oil boom of the 1910s and '20s. Then the Depression hit. Population withered from around six thousand to two." She pointed. "That's our City Hall."

Dex ducked his head to check out the austere double-story Georgian building on the corner. The national flag fluttered on a pole planted in one sidewalk, a single old-fashioned light post stood on the other. Next door was a neatly trimmed park with a bucking bronco monument. An ice cream shop came into view. An old man stopped licking his vanilla cone to peer at the Lexus as they slid by.

Yep. They were a long way from L.A.

"Feel strange to be back?" he asked.

"I'm having one of those 'seems like years ago and only yesterday' moments. That's the kindergarten I worked at."

Clutches of kids were on recess, running around a bright plastic-molded fort and slide while a middle-aged lady straightened a toddler's hat.

Farther down was a café, a real estate office and finally a hairdresser called Designer Elegance Salon. A woman around Shelby's age was walking out the door. Her stride slowed as she shielded her eyes from the sun and examined the car. Next second she held her stomach as if someone had poked it. Beside him, Shelby hands fisted in her lap.

He glanced in the rearview mirror as the woman slipped out of view.

"Someone you know?" he asked as they rolled out of the town proper.

Putting on a smile, she wiped both palms down her skirt. "Everyone knows everyone here."

"And that's a good thing, right?"

"There are a lot of pluses. People tend to look out for one another when bad times come around. Death. Unemployment."

He glanced at her rigid profile. Guessed at her thoughts. "But you have to keep a clean nose?"

"Well, you can try." She nodded ahead. "Our place is a few miles out."

The Scott Springs Ranch was off Quail Road. Dex turned the Lexus into a long drive beneath a big *S,* etched in the image of a curved rope, carved in the massive ranch gate. Soon a homestead appeared…painted timber, porch with well-kept railings all round. Not far from the front steps, a giant oak provided a pool of shade. To one side sat an old crippled tractor. Beyond that was a pond. A series of fenced pastures rolled off to the right and the backdrop of jagged mountaintops was so majestic, Dex's breath was taken away.

What a place to call home.

A man wearing a felt cowboy hat wandered out from the barn. His pace was measured; he seemed cautious but not worried. When Shelby threw open her door and slid out, arms wide, a smile erupted on the man's face. The two embraced while Dex stood back. When he was young, his own father was away a lot of the time, building his empire. A far cry from what Shelby's life here would have been growing up. Money couldn't buy those kinds of bonds.

Finally her father drew back. His pale blue eyes were glistening with emotion. "Now this sure is a nice surprise."

"You sounded as if you could use some company," Shelby said.

"So you flew all the way out from California?"

"I brought two extra guests along with me." She gestured for Dex to join them. "I told you all about my new job. This is my boss, Dex Hunter."

The men shook hands. Dex wasn't surprised by the strength of Mr. Scott's grip.

"Good to meet ya, son."

"Mr. Scott."

"Call me Zeb." He slotted his hands into the back pockets of his worn jeans. "Sounds like things have fallen into place for my girl in L.A."

Dex placed a palm on Shelby's back. "She has people talking everywhere she goes."

When Zeb Scott shot a glance at his daughter, Dex didn't miss the way Shelby dropped her gaze and looked away. Clearing his throat, her father pasted a smile back in place.

"You said two extras."

Dex opened the back door and extracted a sleepy Tate. His legs wrapped around his big brother's waist as Dex carried him over on a hip.

Zeb chuckled. "Well, hello there, young man."

Tate held out his dinosaur and yawned. Zeb took the toy and chuckled again.

"I'm sure we had one of these when Shelby was a girl." He glanced across at his daughter, who shrugged.

"You should never have introduced me to Barney."

"That would've been your mom." Zeb's smile wavered. Dex knew the same look from his dad. Zeb was thinking back, longing for those times when they'd all been together. But then Zeb handed the plastic dinosaur back and ran a hand over Tate's hair.

"I've got a fresh jug of lemonade cooling and there's a nice breeze coming down from the hills." He cocked his head toward the homestead. "Let's sit and get acquainted."

Shelby offered to fetch the lemonade with Tate while the men took up chairs side by side on the porch. Zeb set his hat on the nearby table and wiped his brow with a sleeve.

"You looking after her?"

Dex grinned across at the older man. Guess Zeb Scott was the direct kind.

"Yes, sir. I am."

"She deserves respect."

"I agree."

"Some men say the words, but don't follow through with the action."

"Sir, I know about her engagement breakup."

Huffing, Zeb looked down and shook his head. "All that damn awful business… It tore her up. I'm just glad she didn't end up with that piece of crap." He met Dex's gaze. "Don't normally curse but I could say a whole lot worse where Kurt Barclay is concerned. Makes me sick to my gut to think of Reese with him now. She was like a daughter to me and Cathy."

"Shelby's happiness is important to me."

"Which is why you're on vacation with a woman who is supposed to be your employee?" Zeb dug his heels into the timber floorboards. "You can see why I'm a little confused." His voice lowered. "A little concerned."

The screen door squeaked open. Shelby and Tate were back with a tray.

"Pour mine up to the brim, honey," Zeb said.

Feeling slightly unhinged, Dex sipped his lemonade. When he'd accepted Shelby's invitation to visit with her here with Tate, he had wondered a little at how he'd be received. Never had he anticipated being put on the spot within two minutes of saying howdy-do.

The adults started talking again. It didn't take long for Tate to be telling Zeb all about his stay with Teagan and his life back in Australia. They hadn't coached him, so thank God he didn't mention black vans and bumps on his own father's head. Before thirty minutes had passed, Tate had gone from looking shy to sitting at the foot of Zeb's chair, then to skipping out to explore the old tractor forgotten in the expansive front yard.

"How's your lungs?" Zeb put down his half-emptied glass. "Heard on the news again the other day, Los Angeles is the most polluted city in the country."

She explained to Dex. "I had an infection in my lungs."

"She had pneumonia," Zeb pointed out. "She was laid up for months."

Shelby changed the subject. "How about a special roast for dinner? Honey carrots, crisp baked potatoes."

"She's an excellent cook." Zeb's smile turned thoughtful. "Her dear mother was, too."

"But I thought I'd take Dex and Tate out for a ride before I start in the kitchen," she said.

Zeb asked Dex, "Where are you from, son?"

"Grew up in Australia."

"I've read about your outback and the… What do you call those wild horses of yours? Brumbies."

"I lived in the city," Dex said. "I've only been on the back of a horse maybe a half dozen times and that was when I was a kid."

"Then you got some catching up to do." Shelby moved to

the rail and looked over Scott land that sprawled out for end-
less miles.

"Do you have livestock?" Dex asked.

"Not anymore." Zeb joined his daughter. "But I like to keep
the place in good repair. Shelby used to help until—"

"Until I moved away," she slipped in. "Why don't we get the
bags out of the car and I'll show you and Tate the guest rooms."

Guest rooms?

He hadn't expected anything else. Although when she sent
him a private wink as he rose from his chair, Dex wondered
if Shelby's thoughts mimicked his. Could they get around the
separate bedroom issue, if only for one sweet hour or two?

After a simple lunch, Jeb and Shelby saddled up a pony for
Tate. In a corral next to the barn, on the back of a docile animal, the little guy sat so straight and wasn't the least bit afraid,
even when Gypsy worked her way up to a gentle trot.

But twenty minutes was enough for a first time. Zeb showed
him the chickens and a sleepy black-and-white Holstein cow
that apparently provided more fresh milk than the Scott ranch
could use. Tate sat on a stool and tried his hand at milking,
which resulted in giggles and a squirt or two of success. After
sandwiches for lunch, they took a stroll over to a pond that was
home to a flock of indolent ducks.

It was past two when Zeb had another suggestion. While
Tate threw the last of the bread at the gaggle, Zeb placed a
hand on his shoulder.

"What say we head back and I can show off my coins. I
have a Massachusetts Bay silver. Over four hundred years old."

Tate's mouth swung to one side as he angled his head.
"That's not as old as a dinosaur."

Zeb gave a hearty laugh, a sound Dex had come to appreciate more as the afternoon had rolled on. He might be keeping both eyes peeled with regard to Shelby's best interests, but
he was nothing but encouraging where Tate was concerned.

"Come on," Zeb said, heading back toward the house. "Time

for another glass of Murtle's ice-cold milk. Or more lemonade for those who want it."

Fifteen minutes later, they were seated in a living room that smelled a little musty and was decorated with rich oak and velvet-covered sofas. Zeb's collection was displayed on the coffee table. Tate was asleep against a bank of crimson tasseled cushions.

Shelby laid a throw across Tate's legs.

"I'll watch him," Zeb said in a hushed voice. "You two go for a walk. Or have a ride."

Shelby straightened. "Sure that's okay?"

"More than okay," her father replied as he smiled across at Tate.

They saddled up and took the horses out onto a prairie that was a sea of Indian grass. Shelby wanted to step the horses out but Dex was doing fine setting his steed at a nice steady walk.

She smiled at him from beneath her hat. "Pretend you're John Wayne on a movie set."

"I'm aware of my capabilities, thank you. Driving fast cars, check. Braving the Big Thunder Mountain Railroad roller coaster, check. Being thrown from a galloping horse and breaking a leg in three places—not happening."

"I've never been thrown."

"We won't start now. I told Zeb I'd look after you." He straightened his Western wide-brimmed hat that he'd brought all the way from Rodeo Drive. "He really seems to be enjoying the company."

"My mom passed away when I was ten. I was it as far as kids went, so he focused everything he had on me. Folks speculated on whether he might marry again, but my parents…" Her mouth curved with a reflective smile. "They loved each other in a way that goes on forever."

Then, gathering herself, she flicked her reins and her horse jumped into a canter.

Dex stood up in the stirrups. "Hey! Wait up."

"You're doing fine." A warm breeze carried her words back

to him. "By Monday I'll have you giving the Lone Ranger a run for his money."

"If my rear end survives that long," he muttered, wincing as he adjusted in the saddle again.

She circled back. "Click your tongue. Dig your heels. It's easy."

"Compound fractures aren't easy."

She skirted around his horse. "It'll take us till Christmas to get there if we don't get a move on."

"Get where?"

"My special place."

She slapped his horse's rump and when she cantered off again, this time his horse naturally followed. As he jostled up and down and around, the urge to yank on the reins and plead, "Whoa, girl," gradually faded. After a couple minutes of mountain air hitting his face, some primitive part of his brain actually began to get it…this different kind of speed…the steady beat of hooves. Hell, he could almost imagine embracing this new type of freedom. But what he wanted to capture most was riding on up ahead of him.

Where and what was Shelby's special place?

Soon her bay pulled up beside a monster tree. She jumped out of the saddle and threw the reins over a low-lying branch. When he caught up, she put out her arms.

"Want me to help you down?" she asked.

"I'm not completely helpless."

Shoring himself up, he took a breath then swung a leg over and down onto the ground. He even managed to get his other foot out of its stirrup without falling flat on his face. He was about to fling his reins over the same branch as she had, when his horse reared then bolted off. To the sound of retreating hoofs pounding the dirt, he scratched his head.

"Something I said?"

"She'll be back." Shelby leaned against the tree trunk.

"I don't know. I get the feeling she's just not that into me."

As Shelby laughed, she slid a boot up behind her and set the leather sole to rest on the trunk. She wore a pair of soft blue jeans and a pink gingham shirt that complemented her shape and brought out her natural luster better than any gown she could ever wear—and that was saying something. Joining her, he linked his arms around her waist and stole from her the kiss he'd been burning to take.

She tasted of lemonade and smelled like spring flowers. With the air so clean and a rustle of leaves the only noise, he couldn't think of anywhere he'd rather be, of anything he'd rather do, than make love to Shelby here under the branches of this big old tree.

When his lips slipped away from hers, he felt drunk on the satisfaction coursing through his veins. He swept the tip of his nose around hers then captured her mouth again. By the time he released her, her hands were bunched high on his chest and her breathing was heading toward labored.

She smiled dreamily into his eyes. "It would appear that riding agrees with you."

"Your lips agree with me." He nuzzled the scented sweep of her neck. "As well as the rest of your body, especially in those killer jeans."

"They're work pants."

"They're sure working on me."

He brought her closer until her front was pressed flat against his and her arms were coiled around his neck. "Just how long has it been since that night we made love?"

She cocked her head. "Having withdrawals?"

"I could really do with a fix. You're gorgeous in L.A. but here…"

His mouth captured hers again—and this time didn't let go. It got so heated, he began to seriously wonder if his shirt might suffice as a blanket. All the way out here, no one would find them.

When the kiss finally broke, she sighed and looked around. "I've been riding out here by myself since I was nine years old." She plucked some grass and twisted the stems around a finger as he leaned against the trunk beside her. "I know nearly every inch of this land." She turned around and, with a faint smile, drew a fingertip around an old carving on the tree. "I engraved my name here years ago. I was old enough to want to wear makeup but young enough that my dad would've freaked if I had. My mom was gone by then."

Dex saw another name carved beneath hers, faint now after so many years. He tapped the wood.

"Who's this?"

Her lips tightened. "Reese."

"The so-called friend who stole your guy."

"We don't speak anymore."

"No kidding."

She winced, as if reliving some hurt, then stuck fingers in her mouth and blew out a shrill whistle that echoed over the plain. "Stellar will be back soon."

"But I'd planned to kiss you at least twenty or thirty more times before we went on. It's so shady and quiet." His arms coaxed her near again. "All I want to do is make love to you." His grin brushed her lips. "Then again, what's new?"

But she dodged out of his hold and, playing, slid away from him around one side of the giant trunk. She would expect him to follow that way so he crept around the other. When he caught her from behind, she yelped and jumped around, right into his waiting arms.

He took that kiss and would've taken more except that the blasted horse was back, nudging his shoulder with her big hairy snout. Finally, Dex threw up his arms.

"Will someone tell that nag to quit pushing me around?"

"She wants to keep moving." Shelby grabbed her reins, and in one fluid movement, sat perched in her saddle again. "I'll race you."

It took him an embarrassingly long time to mount and that was with Stellar standing perfectly still, looking at him pity-ingly every other time he bounced up but failed to get his blasted leg over. Finally they were trotting off, catching up to the pink gingham shirt disappearing into the distance.

Though he tried, he couldn't stop his horse from taking up more steam. By the time he reached the old barn where Shelby had stopped and was waiting, he never wanted to say or hear the words, "Whoa, girl," ever again.

"This is your secret place?" he asked.

"For the longest time."

Inside, empty stalls lined both walls. Another large wooden door closed off the far end. A crude ladder led to a quiet loft. The hay scattered over the floor and stacked in one corner didn't smell fresh but neither had it lain there for years.

She tossed her hat and it hooked onto a nail on a post. "It's not exactly the Beverly Hills Hotel," she said.

"It has its own charm. I like the decor. Early American provincial barn, if I'm not mistaken."

Tossing his own hat at the post, looking away before it fell to the floor, he brought her near, tucking his thumbs into her belt and fanning his fingers over the rise of her behind. He looked around and nodded.

"In fact, I feel quite at home here."

"This used to be our land, too."

His brow jumped. *Used to be?* "We won't be shot for trespassing."

"Don't worry. My father sold off this chunk a couple years back. The new owner lives in Connecticut and just lets it sit. It's up for sale again."

"Maybe Zeb should buy it back."

"That money's gone. At least my dad's debt-free, though. Lots of folk aren't." She rotated around and he brought her back to lean against him while she took in their surroundings. "I've been coming here so long. It'll be weird when it's passed on to someone who'll use it."

She found his hand and led him to the back door. The iron latch creaked as it opened and let a warm breeze in.

"See that hill? I used to dream about building my own place

up there. More like a castle than a ranch, with a moat and draw-bridge." She grinned. "I was very young."

"Did you imagine a Prince Charming riding up on his horse?"

Looking out, she shrugged. "Every girl dreams."

He didn't want to ask but, still, he had to know. "Have you brought anyone else here?"

"Not a soul."

"All this time?" Not even the ex?

"No one." She squeezed his hand. "Guess I was waiting to show it to someone truly special."

Deep in his chest, he felt the tug. If she thought he was special, he thought she was spectacular. He'd known women before. Some he'd enjoyed more than others. But he'd meant what he'd said to Zeb Scott. He cared for Shelby a great deal.

When his gaze wandered past her shoulder, he flinched at what he saw hung on a nearby wall.

"That rifle looks more like a club."

"It's just for snakes if they want to get too territorial. And for target practice."

"No shooting apples off heads, I hope."

"I wouldn't recommend it but I'm a pretty mean aim."

"A real-life Annie Oakley."

"Annie was reputed to have said that she would like to see every woman know how to handle her firearm as naturally as she knew how to handle her babies."

He dragged a palm down his face. "Life must've been tough in the Wild West."

"In some ways, sure. But they didn't have all the distractions, either. Except the old-fashioned kind."

Butting a shoulder against the wall, he grinned. "I'd like to hear more about those distractions." He rolled a hand through the air. "Perhaps a demonstration."

She arched a brow before putting her weight on one leg and flicking open the top button of her shirt, then the next. When he began to breathe again and the shirt was completely undone, she tugged the tails out from her belt and turned around. Like a pro, she raised a cute shoulder as she looked at him from beneath her lashes and, opening her shirt, skimmed the shirt to and fro, inch by inch, down her back. When the fabric dropped to the ground, Dex physically shook himself and blew air out between his lips, horny stallion style.

"I hope that's not the end of the show."

"I need help." She rotated around to face him. "With my boots."

She backed up to steady her weight against a stall door. When she stuck out her right leg, he knelt before her and wrapped one palm around the dusty leather heel, the other over the toe. The boot finally came off with a pop. He fell back on his saddle-sore butt.

She smothered her grin. "If this is too much for you…"

"Just give me that other boot already."

This one was even harder to get off.

As he tugged at her leg, she laughed. "You'd never make a cowboy."

"I don't give in." He grunted, pulled. *"Easily."*

That boot popped, too. But he didn't land on his behind this time. Rather, he tossed the leather aside, straightened to his full height and found her belt. With a deft jerk, he unbuckled it, then whipped the strip out from its loops. While she blinked up at him, his palms sculpted down her bare sides as his head lowered over hers.

Shelby thought it felt more like a year than a week since he'd held her this close. As he kissed her thoroughly, scooping his hands over her hips then down the inside of her jeans, she set to work unbuttoning his shirt. His jerking and shaking told her he was heeling off his boots, which were, thankfully, less stubborn than her own.

She eased her lips away and led him into a stall. From a

blanket box she brought out a quilt she kept there for chilly afternoons and laid it on a soft patch of hay. She held out her hand.

"Come lie with me."

He took her hands and together they dissolved onto their makeshift bed.

His kisses were so thoughtful and tender that emotion rose to tickle behind her nose and her eyes. When her breath gave a lurch in her throat, he must have guessed that—being here with him in this place, in this way—had left her a little over-whelmed. As her eyes drifted shut, he dropped a single kiss on each lid before his mouth skimmed down to find her lips again, parted and welcoming.

Without disturbing their kiss, she slid her jeans and under-wear off her legs. He did the same. Then he curled over her and kissed her quivering belly, then her breasts still cupped in a white lace bra. Finally his tongue trailed up the line of her throat. Gently he sucked a throbbing pulse point and liquid heat rushed to the heart of her and pooled. As she sighed out a breath, he rolled onto his back. She found herself swept up so that she straddled him, her thighs draped over his.

Warm strong fingers rode up over her ribs. As she leaned in, he weighed and stroked her breasts before he scooped both out of their cups; the surrounding lace pushed them together and up. With his palms oh-so-lightly brushing the nipples, she shifted to lower her chest over his head. As he drew one nipple into his mouth, his hand smoothed down her front until his touch pressed over her pubic mound then slid between the opening at her thighs.

She was slung over him on her hands and knees. As his fin-gers explored her folds and his tongue teased that nipple, she moved her hips, her shoulders, and gave herself over to the thrill. The sensations grew ever deeper, flashed even hotter. When he began flicking and circling that most sensitive part of her, she held on for as long as she could before her body began to tense and burning pressure started to build and condense.

She needed to come—but not yet.

She reached for his jeans. Finding a foil wrap inside his wallet, she brought out the condom and rolled it over his shaft. Then she maneuvered until she was poised at the right angle above him. She snapped the clasp at her back and her bra dropped away.

His gaze was dark and hungry as his splayed hands trailed up the outside of her arms, along her shoulders to her cheeks. And as she studied his face—his hooded eyes, proud nose, strong shadowed jaw—she knew the decision to bring Dex here was the right one.

This structure had been her greatest place of pleasure as well as her deepest source of shame. Next time she visited, chances were this block of land would be sold. If this was her last time, she wanted only happy memories. Healing thoughts. And having this man envelop and adore her here this way was more than she could have hoped for.

He gripped her hips and guided her down onto his erection, more and more until he filled her. Closing her eyes, she concentrated on the glorious rhythmic rub. The push and pull created a glowing friction that quickly lit a flame. With her palms braced on his chest, she rocked more against him, shifting her position enough for each thrust to achieve maximum sensation, hopefully for them both.

As their pace increased, the flame sizzled its way up one very short fuse. Looking down into his face, at that broad bronzed beautiful chest as muscles rippled and crunched, this time she couldn't stop the conflagration.

She threw her head back as shining bullets shot through her veins and embedded in her core. Quivering with contractions about to break, she hunched down into herself and let go. That pulsing kernel of heat exploded. Clinging on to his chest, thighs squeezing in over his, she shuddered as a delicious deep wave crashed over her and she was swept away.

Eleven

"**Y**ou're looking for something?"

Dex was zipping his jeans as he watched Shelby, wrapped in that light blanket, gazing out the stall window she'd opened a moment ago.

"No." Her back to him, she shook her head. "Not really."

Closing the distance between them, he held her shoulders and traced his lips up the slope of her neck to her ear. Those times after making love with Shelby, he'd been left with a delicious buzz humming through his blood. He'd felt sated. Lucky. But this time, it was different. It was...*special*. She'd invited him into her private little world, so different to anything in his, and he'd appreciated the sentiment in a way that warmed his bones. That left him thinking of a next level.

Not marriage. That leap was a long way off for him. But perhaps after everything had settled down and Tate had returned to Sydney, he could ask if Shelby wanted to stay on. Live together. A huge jump for him. Now the idea of sharing his life that intimately with another person both frightened and excited him. And if it didn't work out...

He dropped a kiss on her temple.

He wouldn't think that far ahead. Things had a way of working out, even if sometimes that meant moving on. If it came to that, Shelby had survived one breakup—a doozy from what he could make out. If their relationship soured, well, they were adults.

Hell, she might not even want to live with him.

He bundled her up in his arms. "So whatcha looking at?"

"Many years ago, I rode out here one morning and found a fawn tucked in below that brush just over there." She pointed to a dense thicket. "She was so young, and those big gorgeous eyes stole my heart in a second. I just sat back here, watching, waiting for her mom to come get her. The fawn would push up to stand and call out to her mom for a while then lie back down. When I crept out there to check on her, she'd lay flat down in the grass, like she was dead, not moving an inch."

"Survival mechanism," he guessed, peering out, imagining the fawn and an enchanted Shelby.

"When it got on past noon, I started to worry. I didn't know what to do. I wanted to bring her home but what if her mama came back. I decided to ride back and get my dad. He'd know what to do. But he wasn't happy with me. You see I'd forgotten that my mother was leaving to see her sister in the next state. My aunt was having her first baby."

"You didn't want to go with your mother?"

"I was supposed to pack some things that morning. But now I only wanted to keep that fawn safe. My mother had waited until I got back." Shelby smiled over her shoulder at Dex. "She wasn't mad. She was the sweetest person I've ever known. Except whenever Oklahoma lost a major league game."

He chuckled. "So your mom headed off without you."

"We kissed, said goodbye, and she left in the Chevy while Dad and I galloped back here." Her head tipped back to rest against his shoulder. "The fawn was gone."

"Mrs. Deer came to fetch her, after all."

"When we got word about Mom later that day, that was the first thing that popped into my head."

Dex drew a breath, held her tighter. "What happened?"

"She'd said she wanted to make her first stopover on the way to my aunt's by dark. But waiting for me to get back had held her up. She'd kept driving through when she should have stopped. Should have rested. The Chevy hit a post around eleven that night. They said she died instantly, but I sometimes wonder how anyone could know that for sure."

He cupped her head, gently kissed her crown. Shelby blamed herself.

"It was an accident. Nobody's fault."

She nodded. After a long moment, she said, "I like to think that the mother came back for her fawn and they went home to the woods together."

His heart breaking for her, he held her tight. "Honey, I'm sure they did."

The weekend came and went. With Tate enjoying these wide-open spaces, Dex suggested they spend a few more days. Zeb was happy. Tate was happier still.

The three of them went for long walks and leisurely picnics. Both Tate and Dex's performance in the saddle improved. Another added bonus was that the initial bond formed between Zeb and Tate grew stronger every day. After the afternoon ritual of feeding the ducks, man and boy would sit together to sort through and shine Zeb's coins. Zeb even gave Tate a few to start his own collection.

Dex and Shelby had stuck to the separate-rooms arrangement, so it was the afternoons when they spent time alone, usually in Shelby's abandoned barn.

They'd been there a week when, returning from a ride, she and Dex found her dad in the kitchen, pouring a cup of his strong black coffee with four sugars. Tate was vigorously stirring chocolate syrup into a frosty glass of Murtle's best.

"I'm heading into town," Zeb said before pulling down a mouthful. "There's another leak in the barn roof."

"How many leaks have you had?" Dex asked, taking a seat next to Tate who was sucking chocolate off his spoon.

"Eighteen this year," Zeb replied.

"Maybe it's time for a new roof?" Shelby suggested with a grin when she stopped to thumb chocolate off Tate's cheek as she crossed to the counter.

"Old one's fine. Just needs some TLC." He brushed a kiss on his daughter's cheek as she poured herself and Dex a cup. "Keeps a man young, repairing things around the place. You handy, Dexter? I should get you up there in a pair of overalls with a mouth full of nails."

"Sounds…therapeutic," Dex explained. "But I'm not the world's best handyman, I'm afraid."

"Plenty of time to learn." Zeb drank the rest of his coffee and set his cup down. "When I get back from town, I'll show you how it's done."

"Me too, Zeb?" Tate asked, stirring his milk again.

"You can help me fix that loose plank of the porch," Zeb said with a wink. "Roof's a little high for you."

Shelby handed Dex a full cup and sat down. "It might be a little high for Dex, too. There's not a big call for fixing barn roofs in L.A."

"But when you all come back to visit again…" With a contrite look, her dad changed course. "What I mean to say is, learning how to use a hammer and nails isn't a waste of anyone's time." Her dad bent over to retie his boot. With a wince, he caught the small of his back. "Darn arthritis." He withered into a chair. "It's usually worse in the mornings."

"Maybe we could go to town for you, sir?" Dex said and added, "When we come back with the supplies, I'll help you mend that leak."

Zeb slid his daughter a look; Shelby had suddenly become very interested in the jug of milk sitting in the center of the table.

"No. It's fine. I'll go to town," Zeb said.

Dex looked between the two and joined the dots. Shelby didn't want to risk bumping into Reese. But he'd be there, walking right alongside her. Today was as good a time as any to show the world of Mountain Ridge that she'd moved on.

"I'd really enjoy seeing the town," he told her with a supportive look.

"You saw it when we drove in."

"Not the hardware store," Zeb said.

Dex had a feeling Shelby would know her way around one, too.

She studied the depths of her cup before her frown turned into a stoic smile.

"I have to go to town anyway," she said, "to get some supplies. I ran out of shampoo this morning. We need more coffee, too."

"And chocolate," Tate chipped in.

Arthritis apparently gone, her dad pushed out of the chair. "Let me get my list together. Can you drive a shift, son? Save using the rental."

"I can drive a shift," Dex replied.

"Pickup's keys are on the dash."

When Zeb left the room, and Tate downed his milk then followed him, Dex willed Shelby to look over at him, which she eventually did.

"It's not a new truck," she said. "It's got a few dings in the back. Maybe I should drive."

So she'd be in charge of a quick getaway?

He reached across and held her hand. Her father obviously hoped Shelby would face up to her fears before leaving Mountain Ridge again. He did, too. But, "Are you okay with us doing this?"

She sent over a playful frown. "Well, sure. Why wouldn't I be?"

As Shelby strolled off to find her tote, Dex sat back in his chair. He had screen-tested a lot of actors in his time and that lie had to be one of the best performances he'd ever seen.

As Dex helped her out of the pickup, he nodded at the cotton dress she'd changed into before driving into town.

"That color suits you," he said. "Tangerine."

Remembering their amazing time spent in her secret place earlier, she tilted her head and smiled. "You look mighty fine, too."

His brows fell together as he tipped closer. "Do people really talk like that around here?"

"You can pick 'em easily enough. They're usually chewing tobacco and wearing six-shooters to chase off marauders. In fact—" she pretended to study him "—a straw of hay between your teeth might help you blend in more."

He ran a thumb and finger around the rim of his hat. "I got a fair-dinkum Stetson sitting on my head, ain't I?"

"Fair-dinkum?"

They headed off down the pavement. Already some heads were turning.

"Aussie for authentic. Real. You ought to see *my* hometown sometime. Foreigners still expect to find kangaroos bouncing down the main streets."

"And Crocodile Dundee wielding his knife."

"These days you're way more likely to see Hugh Jackman playing with his kids at Bondi."

"Do you surf?"

"I surf some."

"Bet you look sexy, riding a wave." Her lips twitched. "In fact, you look pretty sexy now."

"If you're trying to butter me up to get in my pants, you should know that I'm absolutely available."

When he tried to nuzzle her neck, she laughed and slapped his chest.

"Maybe not in the middle of town, cowboy."

"What? You shy? I'm sure I have an app to help that."

He whipped out his cell, pretended to thumb a few buttons before swooping his arm around her and grazing his jaw up her cheek while she wiggled and blushed. If people weren't looking before, they sure as hell were now.

She knew what Dex was doing. She'd been apprehensive about coming into town, showing her face after that incident. Dex was letting her know, as well as the rest of the town, that she didn't need to feel awkward about that failed love affair. That was yesterday, this was today. She felt good about pulling up her strides and taking up her father's veiled challenge to come into town. And she was enjoying this play tussle…having Dex bring out into the open what they felt for each other. Which was comfortable and physical and all those things she had wondered if she'd ever feel again.

Still fooling around with Dex, she managed to yank his hat down over his eyes and break away. Dragging the "ten-gallon" back up, he chuckled. "You're on notice. As soon as we get home, and I've helped your dad with the roof and we've eaten that superb roast dinner you promised…"

His words faded as Shelby caught sight of a woman across the street. But the pounding fist that had pushed up her throat soon dropped again. The sudden heat faded from her cheeks. She'd been mistaken. It wasn't who she'd thought.

Dex was holding her shoulder. "Hey, you okay?"

She tacked up her smile and, exhaling that pent-up breath, pretended to check out the cloudless blue sky. "I should have worn a hat. That sun's still got some heat in it."

He wasn't prepared to let it drop.

"When we drove in last week, there was a blonde walking out of the hairdresser. You seemed to know her."

Her cheeks heated as they started walking again. "It's a small town, remember?"

"Was that your friend Reese?"

She didn't want to go into that here. *"Look."* Diverting his attention again, she waggled her finger at a shop front. "Here's the hardware store."

Inside, the familiar smells of paint thinner and freshly sawn lumber drifted into her lungs. Behind the cluttered counter, Mr. Oberey, the store's owner, recognized her at once. He rubbed his palms down the front of his calico apron.

"Mighty-my, how are you, young lady? I heard you'd left us all to go to California."

"Over two months ago," she replied, happy that no one else was in the store. Mr. Oberey had been there that final night when she'd made a fool of herself but he'd only bowed his head as she'd stumbled out of the room. His wife, Millie, however, was one of the biggest gossips in town. Street corners, church lunches, bongo drum recitals—if there was juicy news around, she was spreading it.

Shelby introduced Dex Hunter as her friend and—God bless Mr. Oberey—he never batted an eye.

"So, what can I get for you?" The older man came around the counter. "Or should I say, get your father."

Dex was stroking his chin, perusing the hammers as if they were some strange species from another galaxy.

She answered Mr. Oberey. "Dad's repairing the barn roof."

On a nearby wall hung rows of plastic packets containing nails. His finger slid across them before he wiggled a packet off its hook. "Tell him to try these. Remind him my grandson would be more than happy to do a complete reroofing for a darn good price."

Mr. Oberey turned his attention to Dex. "You liking our little patch of the world?"

"So far, I'm enjoying my stay very much—" he flicked Shelby a cheeky look "—particularly the barns."

"I came here forty-one years ago come April. I was passing through but then I met Millie and Mountain Ridge became my home."

Shelby paid for the packet.

"It's good meeting you, Mr. Hunter." Mr. Oberey tipped his head. "Maybe one day you'll come for a visit and decide to stay." He winked at Shelby. "We could always have this young lady back."

"Thanks, Mr. Oberey," Dex said, moving forward to slip an arm around Shelby's waist. "But I won't be leaving L.A. My family owns a company there."

Mr. Oberey rubbed his sleeve to polish the top of his key-cutting machine. "Is that so? A souvenir shop?"

"Dex runs a movie studio," Shelby explained.

Mr. Oberey's bottom lip popped out. "Plenty of room around here to build those back lots." He leaned back on that machine. "Remember that one…set in the West but in the future. Gun-slingers and cyborgs all wrapped into one." He straightened his apron. "If you made one of them out here, I could be an extra. No charge."

Dex shook Mr. Oberey's hand. "I'll keep that in mind."

Back on the street, Dex confessed, "I can see Mr. Oberey, head shaved, all in black, reaching for his holster and growl-ing out, 'Draw.'"

Shelby was about to tell Dex that Mr. Oberey was the man behind the town's monthly movie nights, set up on the high school's athletics field, when they passed the real estate win-dow.

Pulling up, she tapped the glass. "That's my hill. There's my barn." She pulled her cell out of her tote and swiped up the camera app. Leaning against him, arm extended, she called, "Say cheeseburgers," and snapped them both. Then she turned to read the price in the window and her smile vanished. "He can't be in too much of a hurry to sell. That's way above what Dad sold that property for."

Dex was saying that was a good thing for her because she could secretly hold onto it longer when Shelby heard her name. It came from a soft, unsure voice that she recognized as well as her own. Her legs almost buckled as a hot, cold flush fell through her body. An album of images flashed through her brain, rapid-fire shots of two girls growing up, sharing se-crets, falling in love.

With the same man.

When she heard her name again, Dex turned. Leveling her breathing, she turned, too.

"I thought I saw you earlier." Reese Morgan wobbled out a smile. "You look really well."

"Dad sounded as if he could use a visit," Shelby explained in a remarkably steady voice.

"And she brought me along." Dex put out his hand and the two shook. "Dex Hunter. How you doing?"

"Reese Morgan. I'm well." But she didn't look well. Shelby had seen Reese come out of the salon a week ago but her usually bouncy blond hair looked limp and thin, like she'd been losing it in clumps. And her eyes were red as if she hadn't slept in a month.

Reese lifted her handbag strap higher on her shoulder. "How long are you visiting for?"

"Just a couple more days," Shelby said. The truth was, she and Dex hadn't made any firm plans, but now she was thinking it might be time to head back.

"You're probably all booked up this visit," Reese said, making the excuse for her. "We can catch up another time."

"Yeah." Shelby just couldn't work up a smile. "Another time."

"But are you settled in?" Reese asked quickly. "Found an apartment?"

"A nice place—"

"But she's moved," Dex cut in.

"Oh?" Reese looked between the two. "Rent too steep? I've heard that about L.A."

"She moved in with me." He named the hotel. "My beach house is being renovated."

Reese's strap slid down her arm. "*Beach* house?"

"Santa Monica," Dex said. "Ever been there?" Reese managed to shake her head. "You'll have to fly out. Drop in."

Reese's stunned look changed until a hint of personal pride

flashed in her dark brown eyes. "Are you going to the dance tomorrow night?"

"Are you?" Shelby countered.

"Probably not. That is to say…Kurt's feeling under the weather."

Shelby's reply was monotone. Dead.

"I'm so sorry to hear that."

"I'm picking up some fresh ingredients for a broth." Reese took a deep breath. Time to wrap up. "Well…it was good bumping into you."

Shaking inside, Shelby let Dex guide her the rest of the way to the pickup. As the engine kicked over and they pulled away, she caught Reese's reflection in the side mirror.

Reese was leaning against the glass window, watching them drive away. Shelby couldn't help but think that, with her wispy pale hair and chalky complexion, more than in that photo, her old friend truly looked like a ghost.

That night after dinner, when Tate had been tucked in, Dex was primed to get to the heart of the Reese/Kurt mystery. He bided his time while he, Shelby and Zeb sat together out on the porch, discussing how the roof repairs had gone that afternoon. Dex had enjoyed standing atop of the ladder, handing over nails and listening to the echoing thud of the hammer. He liked the reward of helping to mend what was broke.

When Zeb rose from his chair and nodded a goodnight, Dex saw the approval in the older man's gaze. It said, *I'll make a country boy out of you yet.*

As soon as Zeb was well out of earshot, Dex put it to Shelby. "Why did you leave Mountain Ridge?"

She blinked twice then looked away. "All my life, I minded my own business…"

"Until…"

The tension locking her body intensified before it seemed to melt and drain away. She shrugged. "Until a year ago, when I met someone. A man. *That* man."

Looking around the front yard, with its derelict tractor and ancient oak tree, Dex lowered his voice to ask, "He wasn't from around these parts?"

"He said he'd lost his family, except for a sister he didn't see. He wanted to settle in a small, close-knit town. He had experience in saddlery and wanted to set up a shop. There was a lot of talk, very convincing. It was easy to listen." She sat up straighter. "We got closer. You know, started dating. After two months, he asked me to marry him."

Dex couldn't take his eyes off her profile, so beautiful and proud. Suddenly so haunted.

"I know you're thinking two months is quick," she said. "But he had that way about him. For the first time I saw my life shining out before me into a bright happy future. I'd fall asleep thinking how lucky I was that he'd come wandering through my town rather than some other girl's. How blessed I was that he'd met me."

"Your dad approved?"

"Kurt did the conventional thing. He asked to speak to my father alone. When they walked out from the drawing room, Dad gave his blessing. But his expression was…"

"Suspicious?"

"Sad."

She pushed out of the chair and Dex followed. When she gripped the rail, his hand folded over hers. Below them lay an uncared-for flower bed. The ground was weeded over, with a few chicories pushing up high between the stones.

"I've wondered since," she said, "what my mother would have said. She only ever wanted me to be happy and Dad knew I wouldn't be happy with Kurt. Later, when it all ended, he said he'd read it in Kurt's eyes. Calculating lizard eyes, he called them. I didn't see that at all. Not in those first weeks."

Dex gently prodded. "So he gave you a ring."

"Kurt said he had to fix up his finances first." She flicked him a glance. "He said he had a property in New York State. As soon as his money was through, he promised he'd put the biggest, most beautiful diamond on my finger. I didn't care about diamonds. I only wanted to be joined with my soul mate. The person who seemed to understand me like no one else could." A sweep of hair fell over her face as she bowed her head. "This must make you uncomfortable."

Normally he tried to avoid uneasy feelings. Much easier to laugh at life than cry over it. But he'd wanted to hear this story for a long time...all of it. He wanted to at least try to understand. And he thought she might want that, too.

"We were planning which part of the ranch Dad would give us as a wedding present," she went on. "When Kurt pointed out we should be given the best acres because my father would leave it all to us one day anyway, I admit, my stomach rolled over. But instead of listening to intuition, I scolded myself. I shouldn't be so judgmental. Kurt was only being practical. I'd found someone I wanted to spent my life with. I didn't want to get all defensive, pushy and run him off."

"Then you got sick?"

"Right after my father had the documents drawn up. I was planning the wedding for the following month when a cold I'd been nursing got worse. I couldn't stop coughing. And I felt so incredibly weak."

"But your dad had signed? The land was Kurt's?"

She shook her head. "Thank God. I collapsed at work. Next thing I knew, I was in the hospital in a neighboring town. I didn't come out for months."

"So dear Kurt shifted his attentions to a new victim."

"Knowing it was Reese hurt me more than anything. When I was well enough to come home, when my father told me before anyone else could, my world was torn apart. For the longest time, I just couldn't believe they would do that to me. But when I was stronger, I took to riding again and I started to see things differently."

"Like you were lucky to have escaped being tied to a two-timing ass?"

"I figured it simply wasn't meant to be. Kurt wasn't the one for me."

Dex growled. "You bet he wasn't."

Her smile wavered and her eyes grew distant as she thought back again.

"They sent me an invitation to their engagement party."

"Classy."

"Of course I decided not to go. I'm not sure why I changed my mind. Maybe I wanted to see for myself they were happy when I was…" She shuddered then went on. "I didn't stay long." She caught his gaze and lowered her voice even more. "Can I tell you something? No one knows."

"Thumbscrews couldn't drag it out of me."

"When I left…I was crying."

Wishing he had known her and could have been there for her, he rubbed her arm.

"I wasn't thinking straight," she went on. "When I got into the pickup, somehow I put the gear in Reverse instead of First. Kurt's car was parked behind me. A spruced-up '67 yellow Mustang that he was always crowing about." She took a breath. "I slammed right into the hood."

Dex only smiled.

"I revved and the pickup crunched out, but my hands were shaking. I couldn't seem to work the gears right."

"You hit it again?"

"Hard this time."

He grinned wider then sobered. "But someone must have heard the smash."

"It was storming. Lots of thunder. And, as I sat there wondering what on earth to do now, a lightning bolt ripped down, right out of the center of the black night sky. When it tore into the tree beside me, I stepped on the gas. This time the pickup leaped forward. At that same moment, the tree toppled and smashed Kurt's car like a toy." She gnawed her lower lip. "I should have told someone."

"About the collision or the tree?"

"I found out later he wasn't insured."

Dex leaned back against the rail and folded his arms. "Couldn't have happened to a nicer guy."

"My father is honest to his core." She closed her eyes as if unable to bear a thought. "If he knew I left the scene of an accident, he would be so ashamed."

Dex didn't think so. Dex thought that if Zeb had been in the same situation, he'd have accidentally put that pickup in Reverse way more than twice.

"I should have gone to the sheriff," Shelby was saying. "Turned myself in."

Imagining the hand of God in that lightning bolt, Dex comforted her. "Greater powers than yours were at work that night."

Not that the score was anywhere near even.

The hoot of an owl echoed out from the shadows. When the moon slid behind a silver cloud, Shelby yawned then shook herself. "Suddenly I feel as if I just want to curl up and sleep."

"It's called catharsis." He took her hand. "I'll take you in."

He saw her to her bedroom, which was on the opposite side of the house from his guest accommodation. At the doorway, he gathered her in his arms and kissed her, light and tender. As she pressed in against him, he thought again of how they'd made love on the blanket in their abandoned barn this past week. Then he remembered how tense she'd been bumping into that no good ex-friend of hers.

But most of all, he thought of Kurt's Mustang and how much it must have pained him to see the wreckage. He'd like to have dropped the damn car on that jerk's head.

As he drew away, she stayed close, twining her arms around his neck and urging his mouth down again.

He smiled. "We don't want to start something we can't finish."

"Can you stay with me tonight?"

"In your room? Shelby, I want to, but…"

"I just want you to hold me." She peered up into his eyes. "I want to wake up with you holding me."

He wondered how many mornings she had woken up re-membering that her ex was playing under the sheets with her best friend. That had to be one of the all-time worst kicks in the gut. No one deserved that, especially Shelby.

He grazed his lips over hers and murmured, "I'll leave at dawn."

Then she took his hand and, once inside the room, he watched as she peeled off her dress, bra and underwear until she stood naked before him, glowing in misty lamplight.

Joining her beneath the sheets, reaching for the lamp switch, his hand grazed a DVD—a rerelease of one of her silent screen idol's films. Dex wasn't Valentino, a national heartthrob who could sweep his heroine away to his tent in the desert or leave her breathless holding her cheek-to-cheek in a tango. But he could help Shelby smudge away her past. Balm the scars.

With his arm around her, he stroked her hair until her breathing was deep and even. When he woke at dawn, which had to be some kind of first, he dropped a quiet kiss on her fore-head and didn't move again until her father's hammer started up outside; Zeb had found another leak.

Then she stirred, stretched, looked into his eyes and gave him a smile that was worth every bit of pain from the cramp in his arm.

When she whispered, "Thank you," and cupped his jaw, something shifted and squeezed inside of his chest. Some-thing he hadn't known existed until that moment. He found himself wondering about leaving…not Mountain Ridge but the movie-making fast lanes of L.A. He smiled at the thought of Dex Hunter, country boy.

Then he pondered the predicament of perhaps getting him-self in too deep.

Twelve

"We have dances every month," Shelby told him as they walked up the path that led to the brightly lit community hall, which was already pumping with music. "Those big movie nights, too. Sounds old-fashioned, I know."

"Not at all." Dex's face turned a little pained. "Well, a bit."

"In a tight-knit community, there's always something to celebrate."

"And tonight it's a solider coming home. A reason to celebrate, if ever there was one."

When, she hesitated, one foot on the hall's bottom step, he stopped, too.

"Walking up these steps…" she murmured.

She didn't have to say the rest. Facing all those people who knew she'd been dumped and replaced by her best friend had to be hard.

Yesterday, after bumping into Reese Morgan in town, Shelby had relayed the full story behind her sudden departure from Mountain Ridge. Dex remembered Reese asking about the town dance. When he mentioned it, Zeb recalled that this month the town had a special reason for coming together—a returned solider.

Dex had offered to take Shelby, if she wanted to go. Zeb said he'd be here with Tate and, as far as Dex was concerned, it seemed like a fitting, full-circle way to end this visit. This time Shelby would leave with her head high, showing them all that her future was bright.

It might not have seemed like it at the time, but she was lucky to have fallen ill and sidestepped a life with a man who could let his fiancée lie in a hospital bed while he fooled around with the best friend. But clearly, this minute, Shelby was swamped by bad memories.

With a knuckle, he gently lifted her chin. "We don't have to go in."

"I need to." Her face lightened. "I want to."

He snatched a peck from her lips. "Good girl."

With his hand on the small of her back, they took the rest of the steps.

Inside, the music was loud but not over-the-top. The giant room was packed with people of all ages; some danced while others were happy to talk. Dex wasn't surprised to see the local band—the Mountain Ridge Rascals, according to the drum skin—doing a fine job on stage; the guy shaking his maracas seemed particularly enthusiastic.

"Big turnout," Dex said over the noise.

Tacking up her smile, Shelby agreed, but that pulse hammering in the side of her throat told him she was on tenterhooks, waiting for some kind of bomb to fall.

"Recognize anyone?" His palm slid higher up her back, lightly bracing her. "Or should I say everyone?"

She scanned the room, her gaze hunting out at least two someones: Reese Morgan and the mysterious Kurt Lowlife. But Reese had said Kurt was sick; they probably wouldn't be attending.

Dex was tapping his foot to a recent pop rock tune when

a prickly sensation scuttled up his spine and the hairs on the back of his neck stood up. He checked to his right then his left. It was like a sci-fi film where the aliens were tuning into the fact there was another among their kind. In a rippling wave, person after person looked their way, and kept right on looking.

Beside him, Shelby stiffened. He was laid-back as far as manners were concerned but this was plain rude. He'd wondered if Shelby's anxiety about facing this crowd had been exaggerated. Now he knew it wasn't. She deserved a medal for coming here at all.

Some of the couples were nodding, looking pleased, supportive. Others' expressions said they were stunned. Appalled. Because of a breakup that wasn't her doing?

Having woven through the mob, Mr. Oberey from the hardware store appeared in front of them.

"I was just saying to my wife," he said, swirling a cup of punch, "I hoped you two would make it tonight."

"Is Mrs. Oberey here somewhere?" Shelby cast an uninspired glance around.

"Putting the finishing touches to the cake."

As Mr. Oberey talked on, Dex's senses homed in on one particular guest who seemed mesmerized by their presence. Standing by a speaker beneath a swag of red, white and blue streamers, Reese Morgan held a tray of finger food. Her face was as ashen as her hair.

The man who sauntered up to her wore a naval officer's JAG jacket teamed with jeans and white sneakers. In Dex's opinion, bad form. They were here to celebrate a soldier's return. Fair bet this guy—his guess it was Kurt—hadn't served time in the military and that the costume had been bought online. The jacket—and its stripes—was a fake, just like the jerk wearing it.

Reese's focus had stayed glued on Shelby. When her lips moved, Kurt's attention shot over, too. Reptilian eyes narrowed and shoulders went back before a leer spread across his face. Dex's jaw set as anger bubbled up inside of him.

It took him a moment to realize that someone on the stage had called for everyone's attention. When the soldier's father began to talk about how proud he was of his boy, Dex paid attention.

The soldier took the mic and a round of applause went up. Sergeant Hugh Evans said a few words—*Great to be home, thanks for being here.* Then he asked everyone to bow his or her head and remember those who would never again share this kind of time with friends and family.

When Dex looked up, Kurt and Reese had vanished and an old dear was handing him and Shelby cake. As the band kicked off again and the lights faded, he forced Kurt further from his thoughts, forked in a mouthful and hummed over a smile. He nudged Shelby. "This is almost as good as yours."

She'd opened her mouth, most likely to deny it, when a third person joined their little circle.

"Hi, Shelby," the soldier said. Then he nodded cordially at Dex. "Don't believe we've met."

Introductions were made and Dex heard how Sergeant Evans had gone all the way through school with Shelby, how he'd always wanted to serve his country.

"But tonight I'm letting my hair down." The sergeant rubbed a palm over his buzz cut. "Or what I can of it. Dex, do you mind if I ask Shelby for a dance?"

Shelby looked torn but there was no need. This wasn't Rance wheedling in on his territory. This was her old classmate, a hero.

Dex stepped back. "I was about to get some punch anyway."

Moving to the counter, he set down his cake and was handed a cup. Standing off to one side, he sipped and smiled, watching Shelby dance and catch up with Evans. Her dress was simple, but that tinkle of laughter drifting over was rich. She might have run away from this place and yet some part of her would always belong here.

That's when the man he assumed to be Kurt sidled up alongside him.

"Nothing like these small-town get-togethers," said the man in a baritone voice.

Dex turned to him. JAG jacket. Stupid smile. The urge to smack this pretender in the jaw leaped up again. But he pushed the impulse back down as he drank the rest of his punch and told himself this was not the place.

"It may be a small town," Dex said levelly, "but there's nothing small about this occasion."

Hands clasped, Kurt rocked back on his sneaker heels. "Agreed. I told Reese we need to invite the sergeant over for a meal. They went to school together." He tilted his head at the couple dancing. "Both of them, too. Although, right now, they look a little closer than friends." If a snake could chuckle, it'd make the same sound Kurt did now...asthmatic and slimy. "I'd keep an eye on that. It could turn into something more serious."

A hand twitched and a fist formed at Dex's side.

Over the music, Kurt chuckled again. "Aw, I'm just fooling with you. Everyone's talking about how great she's doing in the land of the stars. Word is that Shelby minds your kid, right?" Kurt dashed a look behind Dex's back. "Did you bring him?"

Dex listened to this man bleat on like they were old friends catching up; the idea turned his stomach.

But then he caught sight of Shelby dancing with her soldier, laughing at something Hugh Evans had said, and Dex knew a good portion of her apprehension over her coming back was gone forever. No matter what had happened in the past, she was over the hump and that made Dex smile to his core.

As far as the vermin standing next to him went... he'd wasted too much time on Captain Kurt as it was. Even so, before he left, it would be remiss of him not to point something out.

"You deserve my thanks," Dex said.

Kurt paused then looked him up and down. "What for?"

"I know you weren't being generous. I suspect the only word in your vocabulary is "me." But I'm glad you latched on to Shelby when you did. I'm pleased you dumped her when she needed you most. Because you sent her to me and that's

something to be grateful for. Oh, and don't go near her tonight."
Before heading off, he added, "Don't ever go near her again."

The song ended. Dex moved forward as Hugh delivered
Shelby over to him.

"My folks are putting on a lunch tomorrow," Hugh said.
"Be great to see you both there."

Dex shook the soldier's hand. "Sounds great."

As Hugh sauntered off, Dex held both Shelby's hands in
his. "Having fun?"

"Yeah. I am. But I think I'm ready to go home."

"All this excitement wore you out after spending a week sitting on a porch, listening to owls hoot and counting the stars."

"I like sitting on the porch with you." They strolled toward
the door. "Must be getting boring for you, though."

"A change of pace is good."

But he could admit, other than the music tonight, generally
it was super quiet around Mountain Ridge.

Before stepping out onto the landing, she gave one last look
at the party then leaned her head against his arm as they walked
down the stairs.

"I told you that I came to Reese and Kurt's engagement
party," she said as they crossed to the rental car. "It was held
in this hall."

"The night you smashed up JAG boy's pride and joy." Dex
hoped the S.O.B. rode a moped now.

"Want to hear the rest?"

He did a double take. "There's more?"

"You might call it the climax."

Walking still, he wound one arm around her back and let
out a breath. "Go ahead."

"Well, I was focused on being positive—generous—even
when everyone was rubbing my hand and asking if I was okay.
I was the woman who'd almost died and lost a fiancé all in six
months. Before the speeches, I came out here in the fresh air
to compose myself." She indicated a rotunda in the near distance. "Over there, with these two eyes, I saw Kurt getting up

close and 'let's get naked' with a woman I hadn't seen before. I went hot then icy-cold all over. Maybe I was in some kind of shock. All I know for sure is that something inside of me snapped. Then I made a complete fool of myself."

He remembered the night at Rance's and how she'd fixed that story. He cupped her shoulders. "Listen. No one would judge you for letting Reese know what you'd seen." He recounted, "You went up on the stage, on a gracious note congratulated them and then later…"

She was shaking her head. "The way I told it the night I helped you and Rance with that script…it didn't happen like that. I didn't handle myself with dignity and leave a crowd awed by my capacity for forgiveness. I stole the microphone, ordered the music down and blurted out what I'd seen to everyone who could hear within a twenty-mile radius. Then I went on to divulge every detail of our affair, highlighting how Kurt had tricked me into caring for him before dropping me like a virus when I lay in bed close to death and he realized he wouldn't be able to get a hold of my land.

"I explained in great detail how he'd swapped his affections for my very best friend's. The woman I'd grown up with and had loved like a sister."

"And then people came up to comfort you while others strode off to lynch the gold-plated jerk?"

"Kurt calmly walked up onto the stage, gave me a sympathetic smile and announced that he understood about those kinds of sisterly relationships. He said that the woman I had seen him with, the same woman who was standing mortified along with the rest of the crowd, was, in fact, his very own flesh and blood."

Dex groaned. "Damn."

"And then I remembered that long-lost sibling he'd spoken about all those months ago, someone he hadn't seen in years and missed badly. Apparently he'd contacted her about his engagement and she'd shown up to surprise him. I left Mountain Ridge the next day."

Bringing her close, Dex rubbed her back while she rested her cheek on his shoulder. "Yeah, well, he's still a slime bag."

"You don't know how many times I've lived that scene over in my head, wishing I could change it."

"You had guts. Don't let anyone tell you any different. Much better than holding your tongue if you'd been right."

Maybe if he and Cole had risked telling their father about Eloise and her games, it'd save Guthrie a whole pile of trouble later on. Or maybe he'd only look at his sons like a pair of fools.

He brushed a wave of hair away from her flushed cheek.

"Point is," he said, "you're free of him."

"It's a lesson. Now I walk away from other people's bad decisions, no matter who they are or what they've done."

Dex was about to agree when his cell vibrated in his pocket.

When he hesitated, Shelby told him, as she had that first night, "It could be important."

Dex knew Tate was safe with Zeb. Teagan apparently had a "friend" to look out for her. Perhaps the private investigator he'd hired had some news. Back home in Australia, Brandon might have tracked down some important link that had led to a breakthrough in his father's situation. Or there could have been another attempt on Guthrie's life.

Dex connected. As he listened, cell pressed hard to his ear, he felt as if a giant landslide had knocked him off his feet and dumped him flat on his back. He'd been prepared for almost anything but, dear God, not this.

He thanked the officer on the other end of the line and disconnected. Never in his wildest dreams had he ever thought it would come to this.

"There's been a fire," he said.

Shelby's face flashed with horror then she gripped his arm. "Where? Is anyone hurt?"

"My home's been gutted, burned to the ground." Cursing, he threw open the car door. "The authorities want to see me at my earliest convenience."

Thirteen

He stood behind the police tape, glaring at the destruction that had once been his home. Beside him, Shelby held on to his middle as if she were worried he might toss himself onto the rubble.

"I'm so sorry, Dex," she said as a flaming Californian sun rose higher in the sky behind them.

He tried to make light. "It was just a house."

A very fine house he'd been comfortable living in. Had been proud of. But brick and timber could be replaced.

"I'm angrier about what could have happened if anyone had been inside. If I hadn't booked that suite…if you or Tate had been in there…"

Before his studio's latest box office hit, he might have struggled a bit with budgets and trying to placate his brother Cole whenever they seemed to be dipping into the red, but life in L.A. had been relatively easy. Until that blackmail letter had shown up. Since then everything seemed to have been turned around and tossed upside down.

"Is there any chance it was an accident?" Shelby asked.

"Experts will find out soon enough."

"And if they find the fire was set intentionally?"

Then there'd be questions to answer. He'd spoken with his P.I. extensively on the phone when he'd first heard, as well as in person when they'd touched back down earlier. The street-wise ex-cop didn't have any strong leads yet. Surveillance cameras had been installed inside as well as out. Would the authorities be able to trace any evidence back to the perpetrator? If they did, the story behind that other, long-ago fire would surely come out.

Dex rubbed his brow.

What was he going to do? What *could* he do, other than find a good lawyer? And double his efforts to keep those he cared about safe.

"They'll find evidence," Shelby said, her hands weighing on his arm. "Whoever's behind this is not only serious, he's deranged."

Shutting his eyes, wishing he could bury it all, he edged away. "I'll handle it."

"I know it's hard," she went on, "but you have to tell the authorities everything, and tell them now. Things could get worse. You know that, right?"

Under his breath, Dex growled. He'd had a brilliant time with Shelby in Mountain Ridge. He was grateful to have got to know another side of her—vulnerable but resilient... But right now he remembered why he wasn't in a hurry to settle down. Why, up until Shelby, he hadn't been a fan of anything other than short but sweet.

He loathed being pushed. He certainly wasn't ready for a woman to run his life. He had a brain. His own set of rules.

"Dex? Did you hear me?"

He walked away toward the southern end of his charred property. Shelby followed.

"Why don't we get in the car right now and—"

"I thought you were going to walk away from other people's bad decisions, no matter what."

That set her back for a moment.

"This is different," she finally said. "You can't fool around with this. You have to get it out in the open, and fast."

He walked again.

She called after him, "If that friend of yours won't turn himself in, you'll have to do it for him."

"And put him in prison?"

"If he were a real friend, he wouldn't put you in this kind of position."

"People make mistakes."

"Maybe I should invite Reese and Kurt to dinner then."

"You can't compare your situation with this."

Her head tipped at a defiant angle. "Maybe not." She went on, "But you have to go see this friend. Let him know what's happened. If you give him the chance, he'll see he has to come forward before this jerk will ever get off your back. And if your friend doesn't want to step up—"

"Shelby, I *won't* turn him in."

"Damn it, Dex, someone will get hurt!"

"Someone could've been hurt when you rammed Romeo's Mustang."

She had no idea what she was asking him to do. People got over soured love affairs. A stint in a state prison was on a whole other level. Particularly when he and Joel could end up sharing a cell, given that he'd withheld evidence of a crime.

Shelby persisted. "What about Tate?" From Oklahoma, they'd flown straight to Seattle to safely deliver Tate into Teagan's temporary care before returning to confront the escalating problem here. "He can't come back here until someone's locked behind bars."

He held his head. Tried to envisage how the pieces would fall.

"Dex, you have to face this—"

"Okay, okay." He exhaled heavily, then making a deci-

sion, lowered his voice. "I'll speak to Joel. Tell him what he needs to do."

"You mean it?"

He had to see the insurance assessors. He'd contact Joel tomorrow, too. Shelby was right. Last time they spoke, Joel was a sorry excuse of his former self…broke, disillusioned. But it was time to go to the unwitting source of this nightmare and, face-to-face, see if they could put their heads together to work out who lay behind it all before he made his statement to the police. But right now he only wanted to forget all the drama for a while.

They drove to the hotel in silence. Back in the suite, while he poured a scotch and sat on the balcony thinking how different and busy this view was from the Scott ranch's front porch, he heard a faucet begin to run. Then Shelby called out his name.

Before they'd arrived, he'd had the bodyguard thoroughly check out every nook and cranny of this living space. Still, as he moved into the master suite, dread began to creep into his stomach and set in. He had professionals on the case but without any clue as to the identity of the person behind this mess, he would always be waiting for the boogeyman to jump out of a closet. Maybe next week, maybe tomorrow. Maybe today.

Then he saw Shelby, wearing a bath robe and standing in the doorway that led to the attached bath. When she sent him a warm, "I'm here for you" smile, a measure of that bad energy was turned into good.

"How you holding up?" she asked.

"Getting there."

She shook out her hair…ran a hand down her throat. "I feel gritty."

Imagining the taste of ash in his mouth, he rubbed the back of his neck. "*Gritty* is the word."

When she shrugged, the bulky white robe she wore dropped to her feet.

"How's a long cool soapy shower sound?"

Exhaling, he whipped the shirt over his head and wandered over. "Like heaven."

"I thought I could help work some tension from between your shoulders."

He didn't need convincing.

He dragged her close, captured her mouth with his and kissed her like there was no tomorrow.

As his tongue wound with hers, sweeping and probing while her long warm fingers splayed over his sides, down toward his thighs, Dex crushed her closer. This had been a long sorry day. He'd been stirred up by her pushing earlier but, right now, Shelby's special brand of tension relief was precisely what he needed.

Looking like a hobo, his old friend opened the door, clapped Dex on the shoulder then went straight back to the computer. "Got some hot tips for the games this weekend," Joel said.

Edging inside, Dex took in the run-down state of Joel's surroundings. It seemed that his friend's situation had gotten a lot worse since his last visit, which, admittedly, was a while ago. It was hard to believe this man was once a financial mind to be reckoned with. One bad turn in his life, followed by a hard time getting on his feet again…add addiction and finally "who gives a crap anymore" to the equation, and this was the result.

Joel had mentioned hot tips.

"Where do you get money to gamble?"

Dex examined the magazines and empty pizza boxes littering the floor and table, then screwed his nose up at the stink.

"This place smells like a dead toad." And some of the scent was human. "For God's sake, when was the last time you had a bath?"

Scowling, Joel rubbed one bleary eye. "Why are you here? I haven't seen you in so long, I forgot what you looked like."

No point beating around the bush.

"Someone burned my house to the ground."

Joel's gaze widened until Dex thought his eyes would pop

out. When he'd digested the news, Joel resumed his jaded expression and shrugged. "You'd be insured."

Hardly the point.

"Someone knows about that original fire." *The one you lit.* "They want money to keep from going to the authorities."

"After all this time?" Sitting back in his lopsided castor chair, Joel drove a hand through the nest on his head. "What are you going to do?"

"We don't have a choice. We need to go to the police, tell them what happened and let them sort it out."

"Me?" His grin was almost amused. "What has this got to do with me?"

Had he been listening? "I received a note asking for money. Not long after that, someone set a lit match to a mini-coffin in my yard." He cursed aloud. "I should have gone then, straight-away, to the police."

"But you didn't. You stood by me. You didn't rat me out." When Joel's mouth crimped into a gray smile, something scratched at Dex's brain. He hesitated before going on.

"Now we need to fix this."

"Easy for you to say, Mr. Hollywood." Joel looked around at the squalor. "I'm not exactly a man of means anymore."

Dex's frown deepened. Was Joel blaming him for the way his life had turned out? "I did all I could for you."

"Comprising what exactly? A few cash handouts. From a guy who drives a Lamborghini."

Dex's head snapped back. "What the hell are you getting at?"

On a burst of energy, Joel pushed to his feet. "You were supposed to be my friend. When I came to you, you could have given me a job. But, no. You stood back and watched me sink lower and lower. You had a beach house." Joel threw out his arms. "Welcome to my paradise."

"Mate, you have to help yourself. I can't fix this for you."

"Oh, you so totally can."

When Joel sent him a cold smile, Dex froze then staggered back. As the realization fully slapped him in the face, he flinched.

"You're behind the notes?" he asked. "That fire yesterday?"

"You weren't taking me seriously. I had to do something to get your attention."

Dex's chest and throat began to burn. The edges of his vision turned red. "My brother could have been in that house."

Joel held up his hands. "I don't want to hurt anyone. Never have."

"Then look at what you're doing!" Dex's arm slashed sideways. His fist slammed the wall. "What are you? *Insane?*"

Joel's smug expression folded. He rubbed his nose and tears brimmed in his eyes. Finally he ground out, "I can't do it on my own."

Standing here amid this mess, Dex thought of all the years he'd made excuses for this guy, how he'd never ended the friendship when clearly he should have. He'd let this BS ride and ride. And it had come to this.

He growled.

"You get your act together and pay the police a visit first thing, tell them about your problem—" Dex headed for the door "—or, by God, I'll do it for you."

That evening, as he had dinner with Shelby at an exclusive country club, Dex was still stewing over his meetings with Joel and, later, his lawyer, when Teagan called. Immediately Dex thought of Tate and his mood lifted.

"Hey there," Dex said, putting down his wineglass. "How's the kid?"

Sitting across from him, Shelby mouthed, *Teagan?* Dex nodded.

"Your ego will be happy to know," Teagan said down the line, "that your little brother is missing you.

All he can talk about is riding ponies, feeding ducks, collecting coins and how much he loves Mountain Ridge."

Dex remembered riding over those plains then joining

Shelby on a blanket in the hay. A warm smile spread across his face.

"It's a special place, sis," he said. "You ought to visit sometime."

"Sounds as if you plan to go back."

His gut twinged. "I have that problem to work through before I can think about that."

Over the course of a telephone call then a face-to-face when dropping Tate off, he'd told her everything. Teagan knew precisely what problem he was talking about.

His sister sighed down the line. "I haven't stopped thinking about you all day."

Dex recalled the ultimatum he'd given Joel, as well as the advice his lawyer had given, and his stomach rolled over. But there was no going back.

"Don't worry," he said at the same time he reached across to squeeze Shelby's hand. "It'll all be sorted out tomorrow."

"You sound sure of that," Teagan said. "Have you found out who's behind it?"

"Thankfully, yes." Dex glanced around the busy room. "But we can talk more later in the week when I come up to fetch Tate."

Beside him, Shelby frowned while Teagan's tone changed from concerned to puzzled. "Tate doesn't need to be shunted around any more than he already has been. He can stay here for a while."

"You have a business to run, remember?"

"I could say the same for you."

Dex coughed out a laugh. "Forgive me for taking time off."

"You got caught in a trap. Can happen to the best of us. But you need to concentrate your energies on ironing out that mess, not babysitting."

"Shelby will be with Tate when I can't be."

Teagan made a considering sound. "I wonder what Shelby thinks about that."

"She looks after children, Tea. That's why I hired her. That's why she's here."

"Is it? Just saying, you don't have to have Tate around to keep Shelby in your life."

"You think that's why I want Tate back with me?" To keep Shelby? He'd make himself clear. "I gave our father my word that I would look after him."

"I know. Just don't fool yourself that you're not looking after your love life and pride at the same time."

Sitting back, not looking pleased, Shelby placed her palms on the tablecloth as he ended the call.

"You're not seriously considering bringing Tate back here now, are you?"

"You heard what I told Teagan." He'd given his father his word, and that was that. He gazed down at his plate. "Let's eat before it gets cold."

"We don't know what the fallout will be. Who can say for sure that your friend will go to the authorities? What if he gets it into his warped brain to go AWOL and throw a gasoline can at your car next time?"

This should have been a celebratory dinner; today at last he'd discovered who was behind those threats. Only more and more this felt like a last meal. From the start he'd known Shelby liked things done her way. She could be downright stubborn. Yesterday, looking over the remains of his house, she hadn't called off the dogs until he'd caved. She was onto him again now. Hell, she was right. Again. Nothing was final until it was done. But the simple fact was he didn't want to hear it now. And she was talking still, going on and on, putting her arguments forward. Teagan thought he needed Tate in the picture as an excuse to keep Shelby around. In fact, the way he'd been feeling since he'd landed back in L.A., if Tate wasn't in his life...

No. He cared for Shelby. He was just uptight, simply longing for simpler times. That easier life in Mountain Ridge.

He picked up his cutlery and dug in. He had this under control. "This discussion is closed."

As other patrons chatted on about their golf or bridge games over the tinkling background music, Shelby seemed to capitulate.

"Okay," she said. "And if Teagan allows it…if they decide to even let you out of the state after tomorrow, you go and bring Tate back." Her chin lifted. "But I won't be here."

He studied her for a moment. "Shelby, are you threatening me?"

"No threat. You hired me to care for Tate, but not like this. I have a conscience."

"Conscience…" His jaw tightened. "What about trust?" Trust in *him*.

"This isn't about trust. It's about safety and the law."

"Safety and the law. I see. And if *my* conscience began to niggle, perhaps I should drop the Mountain Ridge Sheriff a line to report the driver who left the scene of an accident a couple months back."

Her arms unraveled. "You have no way of knowing what will happen with this tomorrow. Next week. Next month." She leaned forward. "You're speaking too soon."

He sawed into his steak. "No. That's your specialty."

"If you bring Tate here, I won't be around and I'll let Teagan know in advance."

He smacked down his cutlery. "Fine. Go ahead. Alert the whole town. You're good at that." When she flinched, he rubbed his temple where the mother of all headaches had started to throb. He tried to level the tone. "We're not playing small-fry Monopoly here. We're playing with individuals' freedom. In case you're forgetting, mine included." He groaned out a weary breath. "If you could give me your support, I'd appreciate it."

A waiter appeared and refilled both wine glasses while they stared at each other in the shimmering candlelight. When her eyes began to glisten, she seemed to gather herself enough to look around the five-star room as if she were waking from a dream.

"You're right. I'm not taking my own advice. I should step

back," she said. "I might not have all of the answers but I know when I'm licked." She pushed to her feet; the movement sent the silver drop crystals on her cocktail dress rustling.

"Where are you going?" he asked.

"Home," she replied.

He gestured toward the waiter. "Let me fix up the tab and—"

"I mean home to Mountain Ridge."

His stomach muscles kicked. She was bluffing.

He tried his best to smile. "I'm not the bad guy here."

"Dex, although I'm really not looking, you're not the only guy, either."

As she strode out, he glanced around at the filled tables and scores of curious faces. It seemed that Shelby Scott had done it again. She'd drawn the attention of a crowd. If he weren't so floored, he'd give her a standing ovation.

Fourteen

The next morning, after spending the night back in her little apartment, Shelby took a seat at Connor's Café and buried her head in a menu. Soon Lila strolled up, ready with her order pad.

"Would you like me to go through the specials?" Lila asked in a friendly but routine voice.

"I'd like coffee and a big hug."

When Shelby drew the menu down from her face, Lila stalled then jumped in excitement. With a squeal, she wrapped her arms around her friend and squeezed until Shelby could barely breathe. Finally slipping back, Lila cast a cautious glance over her shoulder toward the kitchen.

"If he saw us talking," Lila said, "Connor wouldn't be pleased."

Shelby wanted to say, screw Connor. But she knew Lila had to be careful. Money was money. Everyone had to eat and pay rent. But they weren't causing any harm. Other patrons appeared to have their orders and were seated far enough away from Shelby's table that any private conversation wouldn't be overheard.

"Shelby, you look *amazing*. But you always did. Guess working for a handsome hotshot is pretty cushy."

Shelby thatched her fingers on the table. "I'm not working for Dex Hunter anymore."

"He didn't fire you?"

"I quit."

Without going into much detail, Shelby explained that it hadn't worked out. She didn't mention that, if his little brother were somehow hurt because of the mess Dex was mixed up in and she simply stood by and let it happen, she wouldn't be able to live with herself.

"He did give me a great severance pay," Shelby said, wrapping up. "The whole amount owed to me for six months. When it popped into my bank account, I rang and told him I didn't want it. He said if I felt that bad, I could come back and finish my contract."

"Couldn't you work something out?"

"We've gone past that. But it's not all bad." Or that's what she kept telling herself anyway. "I've decided to go home."

"Oh, Shelby, you're sure about that? All that business with the jerk who dumped you for that friend when you were sick. You were so cut up about all that when you first came here."

"I've been back since and I handled it better than I thought I would."

Of course, that was in large part due to Dex's presence, his support, and she'd always be grateful for that.

Sitting up straight, Shelby smiled for her friend. If she thought too much about Dex, she'd get misty. "Now tell me, what's happening with you?"

Lila surveyed the area again. The other customers were still busy enjoying coffees and meals. Connor was nowhere to be seen. She tipped closer.

"I did it," Lila said. "I got accepted to college."

With a squeal, Shelby jolted up and hugged her friend harder than the first time. "When do you start?"

"I'll give notice in a couple weeks. This is an expensive

town to live in. I need the income. Then, when everything's square, I'm going back to Nebraska."

"You're going home. And you're giving *me* a hard time."

"Guess sometimes moving forward means going back."

"And sometimes flapping your gums means a dock in pay."

The women's attention snapped around. Connor was glowering, his mouth a tight, mean line. Striding up, he kept his voice low so the other costumers wouldn't hear.

"You have work to do."

"All the tables are cleared." Lila straightened her apron. "Everyone's orders are filled."

Connor eyed Shelby. "That little chat cost your friend an hour's wage." Then he said to Lila, "And if you want to go to the union and whine about it, be my guest."

Shelby got to her feet. "We were talking two minutes, tops."

Connor shrugged. "Costly two minutes then."

"Doesn't matter," Lila said. "Two minutes or sixty. I won't go to the union. I won't need to." She tugged the apron strings at her back. "I quit."

Connor blinked then slowly bared his teeth in a smug grin. "You need this job. I know your situation. Bills up to your eyeballs. Join the club."

"Her situation is that she's enrolled for a college degree," Shelby stepped in, "and was going to resign anyway."

"College?" His grin slipped before returning even wider. "You haven't got the brains."

Shelby had taken out her purse. Remembering Dex's rebuff weeks ago, she slid a few big bills out. She had plenty in her account and this was one very good cause.

Seeing the cash, Connor's bulbous nose twitched. He crossed his arms. "It'd need to be really worth my while to keep her on now."

Shelby cocked her head. "Oh, this isn't for you." She grabbed Lila's hand, slapped the notes in her palm. "For your impeccable service in the past."

Lila's stunned expression morphed into a wide smile. She

dumped her apron on a chair and returned with her handbag in a flash.

"Shall we go?" she asked Shelby.

"You can't leave me in the lurch like this." Connor held on to the back of a chair as if he might collapse. "You're the only one here till Evie clocks on." He pulled back his shoulders, his Hawaiian-print shirt going taut across his belly. "This is illegal. Obstructing me from earning my living."

"You could ask Lila about that." Shelby nudged her friend. "Tell him what you're studying at college."

"That would be the law and business." She winked as they walked off. "Catch you in the fast lane."

Shelby took Lila out to lunch at a swanky place so she could enjoy being the one waited on for a change.

Then they took a stroll, window-shopping mainly, although Lila bought a "Welcome to Hollywood" glass stein for her father and an I ♥ Hollywood snow globe for her mother. At a bus stop, they hugged again and said of course they'd keep in touch. They even made plans for a reunion. Lila was another reason she couldn't regret coming to L.A.

Shelby arrived back at her apartment juggling an assortment of emotions. She was jazzed about Lila's situation and having a chance to show up their old boss. And she was proud of herself for having the courage to jump on a Greyhound and come to L.A. on her own in the first place.

But now she was also pleased that she would soon be headed home. After her trip back, she realized how much she'd missed the open spaces and fresh air and that sense of familiarity. Hers was a story that would come up from time to time, but people were so focused on their own lives, who truly cared about Shelby Scott's public moment of misfortune? They had their own triumphs and tragedies to dwell on and overcome.

Most of all she felt down that her parting with Dex had been so unpleasant. Neither had seen the other's point of view...although she could admit that her personality did tend toward wanting to direct situations. Be in control. Clearly at times that had worked against her. If she were less outspoken and more the retiring flower like her mother had been…

Shelby flopped into a dining room chair and looked around. Not so long ago she'd felt as if she were living in a dream. Now she was wide-awake. But she'd always have memories of her time spent here. Snatches of conversations. Recollections of his kiss. His smile.

Digging inside her tote she brought out her cell phone. With a couple of clicks, a list of photo albums appeared on the screen. One was taken that first night with Dex. Flicking through the pictures, she remembered the shop facades and fairy-lit trees. She also remembered how a wind had whipped that old photo out of her bag. A split second after that, Dex had saved her from hitting the pavement. In that moment, as he'd gazed into her eyes, something had passed between them… pulsating and pure.

The next album showed images of that magnificent Beverly Hills Hotel suite. Then there were plenty of snaps of little Tate and Teagan when they'd visited Disneyland. That day she'd known the connection between herself and Dex was real. Little Tate seemed to have known it, too.

When she came across the batch taken on their visit to Mountain Ridge, a knot filled her throat and bittersweet emotion stung her eyes. She pored over the shot of her and Dex standing outside that real estate office window. She remembered feeling protected. Happy. When her fingertip brushed his smile now, her chest tightened so much, she needed to gulp down air.

Dex sailed through life, making a movie here or there, having a good time when he could. Never taking life too seriously, if he could help it. And if she printed this shot off to keep in a drawer or in her purse like she had that other one—

The thought brought her up short. She shook her head. She'd left that old photo of herself and Reese back at the suite on her dresser. Now she'd have to contact Dex to see if he could forward it.

Or was it time to let that go, too?

When she got back to Oklahoma, she and Reese were bound to bump into each other, but the damage done there could never be repaired. Even if she missed Reese's laugh so much, even if for all their lives Reese had been like her other half.

Sliding her cell onto the table, she emptied the few things still left in the fridge. Tying a trash bag, Shelby headed for the door. She'd put this bag outside, get her things together and book that bus ride home. Keys could be dropped off tomorrow on her way out.

No loose ends.

She opened the door—and nearly jumped out of her skin. Dex stood on the other side of the threshold. His hair went a step beyond being stylishly mussed. The circles under his eyes said he hadn't slept the night before. Instantly she wanted to go to him, comfort and assure him. What had happened today when he'd spoken with the police?

"You left something behind," he said.

As he handed over the repaired photo, she was careful their fingers didn't touch.

When his gaze continued to penetrate hers and she began to feel herself weaken, she dropped a glance over her shoulder and diverted the energy.

"I'm just tidying up."

"I need to speak with you," he said.

"Did you talk with the authorities?"

He nodded.

"Did Joel?"

He shook his head then gave a twitch of a contrite grin. "They told me I should make sure I'm available for further questioning."

"Is Tate still coming to stay?"

"Yes. But after Joel turns himself in."

Shelby released that breath. She was sorry that his former

friend lacked the guts to do the right thing but she wasn't surprised. She was relieved that Dex understood he couldn't bring Tate back here with that lunatic still on the loose.

And this minute, dressed in a plain white T-shirt and soft blue jeans, Dex looked more handsome than she'd ever seen him. She longed to reach out and feel the rasp of his stubble beneath her fingertips. She wanted to kiss him, have him kiss her back and in that slow, steamy way that always left her sighing for more.

But when he sensed her weakness and stepped forward, she stepped back.

"I'm not going back with you, Dex," she said.

"I thought you liked Tate." When he stepped closer, his fingers touched hers. "I thought you liked me."

When his head lowered over hers, her heart contracted and she rotated away.

"I like you, Dex. That's not the problem."

His big hands curled around her waist and brought her close, her back to his hard front. She felt the warmth of his breath on her hair… She closed her eyes and sighed as tiny brushfires ignited through her blood. Her breasts suddenly felt fuller, the tips hardening against her bra.

His lips brushed her temple. "This doesn't have to be a problem. I told you. Just trust me."

She wriggled to break free but he held on. While her feminist side didn't approve, her body delivered its own response. Liquid heat streamed through her veins, pooling low in her belly, between her thighs. Where they touched, her skin felt on fire.

Carefully, he urged her around to face him. But she couldn't meet his gaze because even if she did succumb to him now, that wouldn't change how she felt about anything else.

His lips grazed her brow. "Stay."

She felt confused. Exhausted. "Dex, what do you truly want?"

A sultry smile tugged at his lips. "Honey, I want you."

That delicious ache spread until she felt almost too weak to stand. "When I told you last night I was going back to Mountain Ridge, I realized that was exactly what I want to do. I want to enjoy time with my dad while he's alive. I want to ride every day if I please. I don't need to run away anymore. L.A. has been an adventure. I'll never regret getting involved. I'll always cherish those memories."

"Particularly in that barn." He cupped her cheek. "We need to visit again. Whenever you want."

"Dex, someday I want to get married and have my own family and I don't want them to grow up in Hollywood."

His head slanted. "We were discussing marriage?"

"I'm trying to say that we're different people. We're destined to disagree, and about the big things. The things that keep two people together or tear them apart."

He looked as if he didn't know whether to be relieved or offended. "So, you don't want to marry me."

"It's far simpler than that." She tried to smile, be kind. To them both. "I'm saying you need to stay, Dex, and I need to go."

A week later, Dex was back at work, sitting behind his desk and staring at the awards lining the opposite wall when his assistant buzzed through.

"Rance Logins here to see you."

Dex tapped the end of his pen against the polished timber. He'd locked himself away this past week. He didn't particularly care to speak to anyone now. But he'd put Rance off a couple times already.

"Tell him to come in."

The scriptwriter sauntered in looking like he'd finished a jam session. Black grunge T-shirt, matching jeans, bright sneakers the same color as his frames. Halfway through the door, he pulled up.

"Good God, man, you look like hell. Being a pseudo dad taking its toll?"

Dex wouldn't bother to tell Rance that his house had been

burned down, that the police were tracking down the perp. "Tate's still with his sister in Seattle."

"So what of the delectable Shelby Scott?"

Dex flicked away his pen. "I thought you were here about business."

"Sometimes the boundaries get a little blurred."

Dex deadpanned, "I'm not in the mood."

"I got that from the red-rimmed eyes and snarl on your lip."

Dex fell back in his chair. "What did you want to see me about?"

"Ill-tempered. Lethargic, which isn't the same as relaxed. I swear I've never seen you this way. Anyone would think you were heartsick." He swung a leg over the corner of the desk. "Not that I'd blame you. Shelby is one in a million. Bright, beautiful and with that certain nurturing quality that, frankly, does a whole lot for my—"

Dex shot to his feet. He didn't need to hear any more.

Raising a curious brow, Rance backed up toward the pin-ball machine. "You really are in a bad way."

"You've got two minutes."

"That script. Where's casting at? Anyone read for it yet?"

"I have it in hand."

"And this new idea… If you're not interested, I'm happy to go spec."

"I'm interested. Just…you know." He sank into his chair again. "Busy."

"All work, no play? Don't believe it." Rance leaned against the machine. "There's a theater event tonight. Good food, nice company—"

"Not interested." Dex pulled out some document or other from his desk and looked it over.

Rance sauntered across to him. When he didn't speak, just continued to stare, Dex dragged his gaze up and cocked his head.

"What?"

"You didn't answer me about Shelby. Do you still have her on your nanny books?"

"And you want to know because…?"

Rance pushed back his glasses then slowly smiled. "She's left you, hasn't she? Is she still in L.A.?"

"If you must know, she went back home." He swept the document aside.

"Probably best. She's a sweet girl."

Dex remembered. "Very sweet."

"Want some words of wisdom?"

"Please don't tell me you want to give relationship advice."

"I like Shelby. She's a real find, and I would have loved the opportunity to know her better."

"Your point?"

"If you're serious about her—"

"*Look.* She's gone, okay? There's nothing for anyone to pursue. She'd gone back to Mountain Ridge and that's the end of that."

"If that's your attitude, then she's better off." Rance headed for the door. "If you need some company…"

"I won't."

"Proof that change is the only constant."

After the door closed, Dex surged out of his chair to pace up and down the confines of his office. This crawling in his belly, the infernal itching at his fingertips and the back of his neck… He'd never lived for his work, but lately he couldn't settle down to any part of it. Nor did he want to kick back. He didn't want to go anywhere, see or talk to anyone.

Except Shelby.

He poured a shot, downed the scotch then dialed his brother in New York. The same afternoon he'd made his statement to the police, he'd organized a conference call with his two brothers; with their father waist-deep in his own problems, the brothers had agreed to keep this situation to themselves. Both Wynn and Cole had expressed their concern and offered to do anything they could to help. All agreed, too, that for the time being Tate would be happiest and safest staying where he was with Teagan—with security measures continuing, of course.

Now Wynn's assistant said he was out, unavailable. So the kid did occasionally get out from behind his desk. Dex tried Wynn's personal cell number. Same result.

He moved to the wall-to-wall windows and gazed out over the Los Angeles cityscape. He'd always loved the feel of this place. The climate was similar to Sydney; the people in many ways, too. So much energy and opportunity and things to do.

His jaw clenched and he turned away.

Seconds later, he was on the phone to Cole.

"Dex, how you doing? Any more word from the police?"

"Nothing yet."

"They'll catch up with him. Everything will turn out. Don't worry."

Dex felt better just hearing it. "What's happening with you?"

"Taryn and I have just docked at Port Villa. You should see the color of the water. And the people are so casual and friendly."

"A long way from the television scene then."

"I'll admit, I'm not missing it. Not that this is permanent. But, damn, it's a bloody nice break, out sailing the ocean blue with the woman I love by my side." The man impersonating his usually grouchy brother took a breath. "You're coming to the wedding, right?"

"Why wouldn't I?"

Cole laughed down the line at the same time Dex kicked his indoor putting cup out the way.

"I'll be keeping an eye on you," Cole said. "No painting 'save me' on the soles of my shoes before the ceremony. You might get a kick out of the audience's giggles when Taryn and I kneel before the pulpit but—"

"Have you heard from Dad?"

"Well…sure. Just this morning. Brandon is following leads." Cole's longtime friend who fronted his own P.I. firm had joined the push to find the criminal stalking their father. "Experts are looking into the tire tracks of the getaway van. No more attempts on Guthrie's life though, thank God. Although I think this is a long way from finished."

Dex had to agree.

"How's work?" Cole asked.

"The script for our next smash hit is now green-lit for production. The prep schedule will be twelve weeks. Production four to five months." He'd get excited about it sometime soon, he guessed. "Suppose I should enquire about your love life?" There was a grin in Cole's voice. "Although I'm sure there's no need to ask."

"I'm…" Dex shrugged. Exhaled. "You know."

Two beats of silence. "You're not serious about someone?"

Dex automatically denied it. But that wasn't entirely true. He'd been serious about Shelby. Serious enough to ask her to stay. If anyone would understand, it would be Cole in his present starry-eyed state.

"Well…" Dex rubbed the back of his neck, cleared his throat. "There was a lady. It was brief."

"Who is she? I have to meet her."

"It's over, Cole. She's gone home to Mountain Ridge, Oklahoma."

"You fell for a woman who lives in a town called Mountain Ridge? Oh, no. Wait. You mean the handy nanny Teagan mentioned a couple of times?"

"Shelby and I… We got, well, *close*."

He couldn't remember ever confiding in Cole in this way, or recall a time he'd needed to. His older brother never took him seriously. Or was it that Cole took everything Dex had ever done way too seriously? And yet now Dex found himself saying more. He started with how he and Shelby had met, how she accidentally knocked into him, spilled his coffee, how he'd known she was the woman he needed to look after Tate.

He went over how difficult she was to convince to take the position. Hell, he even admitted why. And, remarkably, Cole didn't even sniff when he explained about Bernice and that unfortunate episode in front of an inquisitive evening crowd.

He went on about his growing fascination with Shelby, how he'd kissed her that night and she had put him straight. But circumstances had conspired against them. He'd found himself in Mountain Ridge, defending her in front of her ex-friend, making love to her in that barn.

When he was spent, Cole grunted.

"It can totally get you feeling like that," he said. "It creeps up behind you and you're hooked before you know what hit you. It was like that with me and Taryn."

"This isn't love. I don't want to fall down on one knee and pledge my heart and soul." He thought about it more deeply. "I just don't want it to end right now." Not like this.

"I understand. It's scary at first, until you accept the inevitable."

Dex was curious. "You were so committed to work." To his lifestyle. Long-established habits.

"I'm still behind the company one hundred percent. Same way I'm behind my family. That will never change. But, hey, I guess we all have to grow up and understand that we each are responsible for making our own lives truly full. There's more to being on this earth than board meetings and cash flow." He paused. "Or parties and good times."

Cole wasn't being boorish. He was being sincere. Only none of that advice helped.

"She's not coming back."

"Then get on your horse and go after her."

"And then? I can't live in Mountain Ridge. I have work to do here. And Shelby's not the type to settle for a long-distance affair. She won't accept feeling used that way."

And he didn't want to feel as if he was using her, either. She'd come out of the other side of that tunnel before, feeling chewed up. She knew what she wanted. What she deserved.

"If you want her, love her, you won't be able to give up."

Dex heard the word *love,* but instead of shrinking away

from it this time, he held his breath and let the notion wash over him. All his years as an adult, he'd never given that kind of a relationship much immediate thought. He'd been having too much fun to spoil it by making himself vulnerable in that way. When a guy committed, he needed to do it without reserve. Was he capable of that kind of promise?

"I won't hurt her," he said. "She's been through enough."

"Seems as if you have some serious deliberation ahead of you. And, hell, what do I know? Maybe I'm out of line. Maybe you're just not cut out for marriage."

After they hung up, those words echoed through Dex's head. Reality seemed to be inverted. Dex Hunter wasn't one to genuinely consider settling down. And yet now, sitting in this big bright office with the hours dragging on, it seemed as if he couldn't think about anything else.

Fifteen

When Shelby opened the front door of the Scott family home, she couldn't have been more surprised. What was Reese doing here? And looking so hangdog, someone might have died.

Shelby's first urge was to make an excuse and tell Reese that, whatever had brought her here, she was busy. She'd been back two weeks and was helping her dad reroof the barn. But her former friend looked so stooped and weary... Reese might have betrayed her trust—the basic tenets of friendship—but Shelby was still capable of compassion. As Reese clutched the doorjamb, Shelby stepped forward.

"Do you want to sit down? You look pale."

"I'm not well."

As much as she could, Shelby felt for her. But she wasn't a doctor. She came straight to the point.

"What are you doing here, Reese?"

"I needed to speak with you." Her chin dimpled and eyes shone like she was ready to cry. "Shelby, I'm having a baby."

Shelby felt the slug to her gut. To her bones. But when two

people became a couple and pledged their love, their life, usually they had a family in mind. Shelby certainly thought that way.

All those months ago, when she'd missed her cycle, Shelby wasn't worried as much as excited. She hadn't planned to fall pregnant before their wedding, but if she were, she'd have welcomed a child with all the love in her heart. Then she'd got ill. If she'd been pregnant before, she hadn't been afterward.

With Reese's news now, Shelby would like to be gracious. Say congratulations. But that word stuck in her throat like a dry brick. She'd moved on with her life. She was a thousand times over Kurt. But, damn, sometimes it was hard to forgive.

"There's something else, Shelby…" Reese seemed to get even paler. "Kurt's gone."

"Gone where?"

"The next town, the next state. Away from Mountain Ridge. Away from me. From us."

Shelby held onto the jamb.

What goes around, comes around, they say. But seeing Reese now—so lost and frightened—Shelby only remembered all the other trials they'd been through over the years, from first-grade scratches to dreaming about being best friends until they were gray. This woman had hurt her badly, but no one deserved this kind of payback.

She took Reese in her arms and held on while her friend shook. She might have felt abandoned when Kurt had dumped her, but she hadn't been left to worry how she would tell her baby when it was grown that his daddy hadn't been man enough to stick around.

Reese swiped at a tear rolling down her cheek. "I can't forgive myself for what I did. You were my friend, my *best* friend, and while you were hovering between life and death…"

When Reese bowed her head, suddenly Shelby knew she was completely free from being haunted by those ghosts anymore. Not because her friend was hurting but because Shelby

Scott had crawled through the fire and come out the other side stronger, but human enough to still have a heart.

She took Reese's cool hands and gently squeezed.

But Reese shook her head. "I feel so ashamed."

"Don't," Shelby said. "Don't blame yourself. Life's just too darn short."

Reese still looked stricken. "You remember his sister?"

"How could I forget?" The woman she'd accused of being Kurt's lover that engagement party night.

"Turns out she wasn't flesh and blood at all. Last fight we had, just before he left, it all came out. That's where he was going. To be with her. You and me...we were just part of their plan."

Shelby ushered Reese over to the porch swing. They both needed to sit down.

"Nan and I lost the ranch," Reese went on. "And despite all his talk, Kurt had nothing. He was only with me, with you, to get his hands on some profits. He missed his mark where I was concerned. There were so many debts, we couldn't keep up. When he found out we had to sell and there wouldn't be much left over, he got so angry. He told me everything—then he just stormed out."

It all made sense and yet Shelby couldn't keep her mind from whirling. If she hadn't fallen ill, she and Kurt would have been married. Those papers would have been signed and he'd have been a landowner, a respectable man who'd cheated on his wife with his "sister" the whole time.

Shelby nudged Reese's shoulder. "Remember that car Kurt loved? The Mustang? Before lightning struck and that tree came crashing down..."

When she confessed how she'd inadvertently rammed its hood a couple times with the old pickup and how damn good it had felt, Reese actually laughed before she sobered and folded her hand over hers.

"Shelby, can you forgive me?"

Shelby looked into those tortured eyes. It seemed that her

whole life she'd thought about forgiveness. Looking only forward now, she found a supportive smile.

"What's important is that baby having an aunt."

Then they wrapped their arms around one another like they'd done all their lives.

"I hear you're back for a while, living with your dad."

In the gauzy light, Shelby recognized Mrs. Fallon's bulky frame. Smiling, she got to her feet.

It had been a week since Reese had knocked on her door. Earlier today her friend had suggested they hang out at the monthly open-air movie night. Shelby had asked her dad if he wanted to tag along, but he'd insisted, after three weeks back home from L.A., she could use a night without his company. So she and Reese had met at the high school athletic field along with a ton of other residents. As they'd arranged deck chairs and treats right up front, she'd felt the town's eyes on them both, one pair belonging to Millie Oberey.

Shelby only grinned to herself. Perhaps she ought to work up a handheld sign that announced, *Get on with your life. I have.*

But Judy Fallon wasn't a gossip. She was sweet and patient. Now, at the end of the night after watching two movies, Shelby smiled at a memory. No wonder she and Shelby's mother had been good friends.

"Actually, Mrs. Fallon," Shelby explained, "I'm back home to stay."

Judy Fallon sent her calm smile as if she'd known all along but didn't want to presume.

"Are you looking for something to fill in your day?"

"Like working at the kindergarten?"

The older woman touched her arm. "We've missed you."

"I would love to. Thank you. But I can't do quite as many hours as before. I've applied for a college degree. Distance learning, mostly. I want to be a teacher."

Beaming, Judy Fallon swept her in for a hug. "Any school

would be lucky to have you. Anything I can do to help, you be sure to let me know."

As the kindergarten teacher headed off, Shelby sat on her deck chair and asked Reese, "Want to come back for a hot chocolate? No coffee, right?"

Or soft cheese or certain kinds of fish. Expectant mothers had to watch those kinds of things. Growing babies deserved the very best start in life, particularly when the baby in question would be Shelby's godchild.

Reese leaned on the back of her chair. "I would love to get my lips around a hot chocolate *if* I could stop yawning. I have never been so tired in all my life. The doctor said I'll feel more myself soon. Although I'm dog sure that won't include my appetite. You've seen me eat everything in sight, particularly anything sweet. We really need to whip up a batch of your cupcakes."

And just like that, that big muscle beneath Shelby's ribs dropped and quivered. Even without cues, she thought about Dex all too often…how he'd praised her cooking, among other things. How happy she'd been with him, at least for a time.

And Dex wasn't the only person she missed. She would love to have known Tate and Teagan better. All the Hunter pack, in fact: the recently seafaring Cole and his future bride; Wynn, the solemn brother; Guthrie, the founder of Hunter Enterprises and a man who, it seemed, had made enemies enough for someone to want to take his life. Shelby was even intrigued by Dex's stepmom…so polished and conniving, Eloise might have starred in her very own daytime drama.

But knowing about all that commotion also made Shelby more content than ever to be home. She liked routine, familiarity, predictability. Although she'd learned well enough… life could always throw a curve ball into the mix and shake things up. Sometimes a person simply needed to ride out the bumps and get back on track, no matter how much easier running away might seem.

"I need to see that last movie again sometime." Reese was

polishing a huge apple on her sleeve. "That final scene almost made me cry."

"Reese, you were sobbing."

Reese studied the apple as if she were scrutinizing her reflection, then shrugged. "Must be the hormones."

It was because she had a heart.

So did Shelby, even if most of the time now it felt flat. Next life she'd come back as a tree or a shrub. Plants didn't having feelings. They didn't fall in love.

As if reading her mind, Reese asked, "Have you heard from Dex Hunter?"

Folding up the blanket, Shelby's stomach swooped but she checked that emotion. She wouldn't feel sorry for herself for how things had ended, or blame herself, for that matter. She couldn't change what she couldn't control; man, that lesson had been a long time coming.

"Dex called," Shelby said carefully. "I asked him not to contact me again. No point."

I may never be kissed that way again, Shelby mused, returning from tossing candy wrappers in a nearby receptacle. But just because something looked good, felt good, didn't mean it was necessarily good for her. Although she wouldn't lie to herself.

When she'd woken up that morning here after he'd simply held her all night, deep down she'd known. She was in love with Dex, and nothing like the way she thought she'd loved Kurt. Her affection for Dex was real. Ran deep. It might have been etched like an epithet across her soul.

But he belonged in glittering Hollywood with his starlets and premieres and extravagant movie sets. She wished Dex and his family luck with their problems but, as much as she'd like to, she couldn't help. Or get involved. Three weeks after leaving L.A., her time with Dex seemed like a bittersweet dream.

She'd gone so far as to call Teagan, say she'd resigned and suggest Tate stay with her a while longer. Knowing Shelby was leaving, Teagan had agreed. But as far as Dex sorting out his unhinged friend and correcting past misdeeds, he was on his own. She wanted nothing to do with it, now or anytime in the future.

She and Reese said good-night. The rest of the crowd, too, was leaving the field. With her chair wedged under one arm, blanket under the other, Shelby was about to head off when an image flickered on the giant movie screen behind her. Next second, music faded up…a scratchy sequence featuring violins. She blinked around. Was there a third movie no one knew about?

The screen flickered more. When an image of Rudolph Valentino appeared, swaggering up to a woman in a bar, Shelby froze. She knew this scene, the one where Valentino danced his famous tango, her favorite piece of film ever. But the projection area was unmanned, and everyone, including Reese, was still headed for their vehicles.

To her left came the beat of hooves. She caught sight of a white horse cantering away down the field before a real-life figure moved in front of the screen. A tall well-built man with the posture of a matador. He wore a Stetson—no. It was an Andalusia, the same type of flat-brimmed hat Valentino had worn when he'd danced the tango. She knew because this man also had a striped poncho slung over one shoulder, just like the Valentino character in the film. As he sauntered nearer, she heard the *ching-ching* of spurs jangling on his boots. While the light from the screen threw the figure into mysterious relief, her heart crashed in her ears and her knees turned to mush. Shelby knew exactly who stood before her now.

As he moved nearer, Dex Hunter retrieved the rose held between his teeth and presented it to her.

"I assure you," he said in a deep smooth voice, "it's free of thorns."

Before she could say a word, the rose took her attention. She set down the rug and chair to bring the flower to her nose and sniff.

"This is foil-wrapped chocolate," she said.

"That was Tate's idea."

He'd spoken to Tate about this? Was his little brother back visiting with Dex? Was that madman Joel still on the loose? But first things first.

"What are you doing here dressed like that?" she asked.

"I've come to take something from you." His arm snapped around her waist. "A dance."

With his nose touching hers, she stuttered.

"S-Sorry...what did you say?"

His familiar heat and sinewy strength suffused her skin, shooting straight into her bloodstream. She pressed her palms hard against his white billowy shirt but every cell in her body begged her to lean closer, not shove him away.

"Dex, this is sweet, so totally unexpected, but—"

He touched a fingertip to her lips and she fell silent. Turning his head to the left, he seemed to address the air.

"Music, Maestro."

Crackling echoed through the speakers before those violins resumed their vintage serenade and Dex's face drew close again. As those ravenous tawny eyes peered down into hers, one eyebrow arched.

"Do you know the tango?" he asked.

"You mean know it in that film?" The one playing at his back.

"Do you know how to do it?"

"I don't know anyone who actually performs the tango unless they're a dance instructor or on a talent show or possibly an eccentric—"

He pressed his finger to her lips again. "You ask who would know how to dance the tango, the first dance of love?" In the moonlight, she saw a sultry smile hook his mouth. "I do."

"Dex, the hokey pokey would trip you up."

One palm latched onto her behind. As the other caught her side, he arched her carefully back, all the way until her right leg and her sneaker lifted into the air.

"I warn you." So close, his lips teased her. "Resistance is futile."

She coughed out a laugh, tried to shake her brain. But he was already tipping her back up to stand on two feet. In the next heartbeat, he twirled her around and tipped her back the other way. She let out a cry as a leg shot up again.

He'd definitely lost his mind.

"You're making me dizzy."

"Your head is spinning?" His eyebrow arched again. "This is what I planned."

Righting herself, she tried to even her breathing as she shimmied away.

"Reese isn't in on this, is she?"

"No one knew. I only bribed the guy who presses Play on the DVDs ten minutes ago."

Shelby got back on track. She needed to set him straight once and for all. She wouldn't change her mind, no matter how many chocolate roses or tango dips he gave her.

"Dex, I'm home to stay. I'm not interested in a long-distance romance. My life is here. Yours is in California." Gazing into his eyes, she sighed. "If you truly care, don't do this to me. Don't try to drag it out." A ball of emotion lodged in her throat. "I'll only end up hurt."

His expression shifted from playful to pensive. His hand went to the Andalusian hat then he studied the black-and-white screen behind him. Valentino was in full swing, captivating his partner with his moves and with his eyes. When Dex's attention returned to her, his gaze roamed her face with an intensity that sent a shiver racing up her spine.

"Dance with me," he said. "Let me hold you. I promise I won't try to seduce you."

"You are so lying."

"You're right. I intend to do everything in my power to sweep you off your feet."

His arm went around her again, this time slowly but with equal purpose.

"Dance with me," he said again.

She held her breath and then sighed it out. With that devilish smile warming his eyes again, he straightened. Then, left hand clasped around her right, he shot out their arms and strutted forward, tango-style.

She pulled away. This got more and more freaky.

"When did you learn to do that?"

"Lessons every day, twice a day."

A pit wedged in her throat grew. She blinked back the mist coming over her eyes.

"You did that for me?"

"I did it for us."

He wound her extra close again and, caught in the tide, she began to move with him. Let him lead. When he abruptly swung around, about-face, warming up to the tune, she spun, too.

He directed her through the steps, which he performed with remarkable grace and ease. He tripped up once but glossed over it and continued on. He didn't seem the least self-conscious, and even as she felt a handful of people looking on from the boundary of the playing field, she didn't feel self-conscious, either. She felt changed. Free. She hadn't had this much fun since—

Well, since they'd last been together.

As he tipped her back in that dramatic pose again, his head bent over hers.

"I miss you every day. So much," he told her.

Only this time there wasn't a hint of humor in his tone, in his face. He was dead serious and the realization left her feeling as if the ground had been snatched away from beneath her feet.

When the music stopped, his palm ironed down her back. As fingers reached the rise of her behind, he coaxed her in, unforgivably close.

"When I first saw you, I knew I'd found someone special. Unique and proud and strong and fragile all at the same time. I wanted you then. I haven't stopped wanting you. And I realized something else, too."

He took a moment, then continued. "I'm in love with you. I'll do anything to have you. Keep you. I'd dress up in this costume. I'd learn to swoop and twirl. If it means waking up to your beautiful smile every morning."

Shelby felt tears coming on. She worried if she spoke, she wouldn't be able to stop them. But maybe she hadn't understood properly. She had to hear those words again. Had to be sure.

"You said…" She drew down a deep breath. "Dex, you *love* me?"

"Ask yourself. Would I be here doing this if I didn't?"

But even if that were true, she couldn't forget what was truly keeping them apart. "Your firebug friend..."

"Joel finally turned himself in. He has a stint in state prison ahead of him."

Relief flooded Shelby's system. "Thank God," she murmured. "And you?"

Dex had withheld information relating to a crime.

"My lawyer's done a deal with the prosecution. My testimony on the stand in exchange for no charges."

An enormous weight was lifted off her shoulders. "You don't know how happy I am to hear that."

"Then you'll dance with me again?"

She swallowed deeply. "Dex, I'm not going back."

"Then I won't, either."

"You have a company to run. A family company. You would never just walk out and let them down like that."

"Then how about a compromise?"

"I've already told you. A long-distance affair won't work."

"We can divide our time between L.A. and Mountain Ridge. There's work I can do from here. I might even make a set and film that Western Mr. Oberey from the hardware store is so keen on." His grin faded into a loving smile. "Point is, if we want this—us, together, forever—we can make it work."

Shelby was gaping. If he was serious…if he really meant what he'd just said…

"You'd really change your life that much for me?"

He gathered her close. "You are my life. I want to be a good husband. Your husband." His brow touched hers. "And when you're ready, I hope to be a father."

"Pushing strollers? Filling bottles?"

This was all going too fast.

"I bought the property next door to your father's."

"You bought my place?" A tear dropped down her cheek. "With my barn?"

"I'm going to build there. Maybe not a castle," he teased. "But a big family home." That somber look darkened his eyes. "I'm asking you to be my wife."

She coughed out a laugh. "You can't expect me to stand here and believe all this when you must know that—"

Her words were drowned when his mouth captured hers with a kiss that was both penetrating and heartfelt. Simply, utterly, made-in-heaven divine. She was aware of his thumb pressing on the base of her spine, the rhythm of his tongue as a hand steadied the back of her head. All her life she'd been tall. Now she was soaring.

Too soon his lips left hers. When she dragged open her eyes and saw the satisfaction calming his face, she was left stunned.

"I was never going to do this again."

"It's okay." He wound a wave of hair away from her cheek. "I forgive you."

She coiled her arms around his neck.

"I forgive me, too."

"I pledge to love and adore you, as well as your cupcakes and roasts," he vowed. "And there's also that little matter of being faithful to only you for the rest of our lives." His lips grazed hers. "I can't wait." He pretended to frown. "Now isn't there something you'd like to tell me?"

More tears fell. "Do I have to say it aloud?" Surely he knew.

"These past weeks I've daydreamed about hearing you say it."

A thrill ran through her. She couldn't believe this was happening. That she would truly get a fairy-tale ending. She was going to be one of the lucky ones.

"I love you," she said. "Everything about you. And I do want to have children. I think I want that more than anything."

"I've heard that the fastest way to fall pregnant is to have lots of sex. Experts aren't sure about the best position so we should probably try them all."

His cheeky smile faded into an expression that warmed her heart a hundred ways.

"We're going to have a fabulous life together."

She brought herself closer. "We really can do this, can't we?"

Before he kissed her again, Dex murmured against her lips, "Baby, we'll be a smash hit."

Epilogue

Meanwhile in New York...

As Wynn Hunter peeled the shirt off his back and entered his Park Avenue penthouse bedroom, he recalled his night… the boring business dinner, a nightcap at a club then a chance meeting with a woman who seemed as hell-bent on forgetting past regrets as he was.

And he had a lot to regret in the form of Heather Matthews. She had been the most tempting woman he'd ever known. Stylish, playful… Whenever they'd touched, Wynn had felt the sexual charge to his bones.

Had it been love? The kind of love that his brothers Cole and Dex had recently found?

Once he'd been convinced. So much so, he'd popped the question. She'd blushed, held her brow. Then, before leaving him to sit alone in that restaurant, she'd declined. She didn't want to get married. Didn't want to be his wife. Wynn had to admit…he'd died a little that night.

While he usually rushed to the office each morning, for weeks after he'd dragged himself out of bed. Nothing seemed to have a purpose. The world might end and he couldn't have cared less because *his* world had ended the moment he'd slipped that diamond ring back into its box.

But in time good sense had returned and, arguably, he was sharper than before. Lately, for the first time, he'd heard the word *ruthless* bandied around the corridors at work and connected with his name. It seemed that the managing director of Hunter Publishing was no longer considered "a nice guy."

Ever since he was a child, Wynn had counted himself as the most zealous of the three Hunter boys. He played fair, gave chances. Had a heart. Those qualities, along with his soul, seemed to have vanished.

Alakazam.

When he'd realized the change, Wynn was thankful. Relieved. Instead of that churning inner turmoil, there'd come an odd sense of calm. Of course that went hand in hand with trading off personal warmth for this cool, almost detached awareness. He wouldn't call it pleasant. A better word was *necessary.*

Now, as Wynn ditched the rest of his clothes and crossed the room, he studied the perfect naked form draped over his bed. Toned supple limbs, a halo of wheat-gold hair splayed upon the pillow. Acknowledging the pleasant stir in his gut, Wynn put one knee and two palms down upon the sheet and curled over her. She quivered as the stiff tip of his tongue trailed around a tight nipple.

He murmured against her flesh, "I'd like to know your name."

"And I'd like us to get under the covers."

When her manicured fingers combed through his hair and her knee bent languidly toward his chest, a series of sparks ignited in his groin and for a heartbeat, as he slid down the length of her lithe body to her thighs, he had a glimpse of sharing something more with this woman than one night of red-hot sex. Of course, right now he didn't want anything more.

Nor did he expect anything less.

* * * * *

Watch for Wynn's story, the next in
THE HUNTER PACT *series,*
coming soon from Harlequin Desire.

REQUEST YOUR FREE BOOKS!
2 FREE NOVELS PLUS 2 FREE GIFTS!

ALWAYS POWERFUL, PASSIONATE AND PROVOCATIVE

YES! Please send me 2 FREE Harlequin Desire® novels and my 2 FREE gifts (gifts are worth about $10). After receiving them, if I don't wish to receive any more books, I can return the shipping statement marked "cancel." If I don't cancel, I will receive 6 brand-new novels every month and be billed just $4.55 per book in the U.S. or $4.99 per book in Canada. That's a savings of at least 13% off the cover price! It's quite a bargain! Shipping and handling is just 50¢ per book in the U.S. and 75¢ per book in Canada.* I understand that accepting the 2 free books and gifts places me under no obligation to buy anything. I can always return a shipment and cancel at any time. Even if I never buy another book, the two free books and gifts are mine to keep forever.

225/326 HDN F4ZC

Name _____ (PLEASE PRINT)

Address _____ Apt. #

City _____ State/Prov. _____ Zip/Postal Code

Signature (if under 18, a parent or guardian must sign)

Mail to the **Harlequin® Reader Service:**
IN U.S.A.: P.O. Box 1867, Buffalo, NY 14240-1867
IN CANADA: P.O. Box 609, Fort Erie, Ontario L2A 5X3

Want to try two free books from another line?
Call 1-800-873-8635 or visit www.ReaderService.com.

* Terms and prices subject to change without notice. Prices do not include applicable taxes. Sales tax applicable in N.Y. Canadian residents will be charged applicable taxes. Offer not valid in Quebec. This offer is limited to one order per household. Not valid for current subscribers to Harlequin Desire books. All orders subject to credit approval. Credit or debit balances in a customer's account(s) may be offset by any other outstanding balance owed by or to the customer. Please allow 4 to 6 weeks for delivery. Offer available while quantities last.

Your Privacy—The Harlequin® Reader Service is committed to protecting your privacy. Our Privacy Policy is available online at www.ReaderService.com or upon request from the Harlequin Reader Service.

We make a portion of our mailing list available to reputable third parties that offer products we believe may interest you. If you prefer that we not exchange your name with third parties, or if you wish to clarify or modify your communication preferences, please visit us at www.ReaderService.com/consumerchoice or write to us at Harlequin Reader Service Preference Service, P.O. Box 9062, Buffalo, NY 14269. Include your complete name and address.

HD13R

Canyon watched Keisha turn into Mary's Little Lamb Day Care. He frowned. Why would she be stopping at a day care? Maybe she had volunteered to babysit for someone tonight.

He slid into a parking spot and watched as she got out of her car and went inside, smiling. Hopefully, her good mood would continue when she saw that he'd followed her. His focus stayed on her, concentrating on the sway of her hips with every step she took, until she was no longer in sight. A few minutes later she walked out of the building, smiling and chatting with the little boy whose hand she was holding—a boy who was probably around two years old.

Canyon studied the little boy's features. The kid could be a double for Denver, Canyon's three-year-old nephew. An uneasy feeling stirred his insides. Then, as he studied the little boy, Canyon took in a gasping breath. There was only one reason the little boy looked so much like a Westmoreland.

Canyon gripped the steering wheel, certain steam was coming out of his ears.

He didn't remember easing his seat back, unbuckling his

seat belt or opening the car door. Neither did he remember walking toward Keisha. However, he would always remember the look on her face when she saw him. What he saw on her features was surprise, guilt and remorse.

As he got closer, defensiveness followed by fierce protectiveness replaced those other emotions. She pulled her son—the child he was certain was *their* son—closer to her side. "What are you doing here, Canyon?"

He came to a stop in front of her. His body was radiating anger from the inside out. His gaze left her face to look down at the little boy, who was clutching the hem of Keisha's skirt and staring up at him with distrustful eyes.

Canyon shifted his gaze back up to meet Keisha's eyes. In a voice shaking with fury, he asked, "Would you like to tell me why I didn't know I had a son?"

CANYON
by New York Times *and* USA TODAY *bestselling author*
Brenda Jackson
Available August 2013
only from Harlequin® Desire®!

SADDLE UP AND READ 'EM!

Looking for another great Western read? Check out these August reads from the PASSION category!

CANYON by Brenda Jackson
The Westmorelands
Harlequin Desire

THE HEART WON'T LIE by Vicki Lewis Thompson
Sons of Chance
Harlequin Blaze

Look for these great Western reads AND MORE available wherever books are sold or visit
www.Harlequin.com/Westerns

Love the Harlequin book you just read?

Your opinion matters.

Review this book on your favorite
book site, review site, blog or your own
social media properties and share
your opinion with other readers!